THE VAMPIRE HOUND

Jim Kraft

For Jean, Jeff, and Matt—with love;
And thanks to Mark

Copyright © 2001 by Jim Kraft.

Published by Troll Communications L.L.C.

ISBN 0-8167-7315-7

Printed in Canada.

10 9 8 7 6 5 4 3 2 1

I

House Call

Slatkin's nerves were as frayed as the cuffs of his trousers. The ferret had tramped halfway across London, and wherever he trod, from Clerkenwell down to the Strand, the bustling city seemed to be throwing itself in his way. Men hawking fruits and vegetables brayed into his face, while the chimes of London's church bells clanged upon his narrow skull. Newsboys shouted, "Winners! We gots all the racing winners!"—a tormenting reminder of all the times—the many, many times—the ferret had bet and lost. Government clerks marching out of Whitehall and tourists pressing on to Westminster jostled him, ignored him, and nearly carried him away. Slatkin lowered his chin and clenched his jaw, forcing his way through the crowds like a soldier slogging through a storm.

Crossing Regent Street, he stepped in a pile of horse manure. *Ain't going to be my day,* he thought, scraping his boot on the curb. *Too much trouble about. Too much for my poor head to deal with.* The ferret rubbed his paw against his furry cheek. What could he do to make the world back off a bit? A possible solution appeared in the block ahead: a pub called The Ox and Pickle.

There you are, Slatkin, there you are. There's a place to calm yourself. There's a port for your leaky boat. Why not pop in for a pint?

It would be nice inside, cool and quiet, the light glinting off the polished brass of the rails and lamps. Seated on a leather bench, he might settle his thoughts and sip his worries away.

Slatkin stood on the street and looked longingly through the pub windows. He slipped his paws into his pockets. Fingers rooted in the corners and seams—in vain; his pockets were as empty as his stomach.

The ferret flicked his tongue across his dry lips. *No comfort for you today, Slatkin. No rest for a weary soul.* The old cough scratched insistently at the back of his throat, and he hacked hard to get it out. *Just as well, I reckon. That doctor won't like to be kept waiting. Wonder if he can do something for my cough?* Casting a last, yearning glance at the pub door, he moved on.

A short time later, his mind blanketed by his troubles, the ferret stepped off the curb at Hyde Park Corner . . . and into the path of a horse-drawn omnibus. For several long moments Slatkin stood rooted to the street, entranced by the sight of his approaching doom. The passengers perched on top of the bus, its portly driver, and its pair of chestnut horses in their jangling harness all came sharply into focus. The words NESTLÉ'S MILK leaped out at the ferret from a placard beneath the driver's feet. *I should drink more milk,* Slatkin thought, as the bus came on. *On the other hand, I'm about to be mashed like a potato.*

The horses were nearly upon him. The ferret could hear their snorting and smell the musty odor of leather and horse. The bus driver stared straight ahead, seemingly unconcerned. *I ain't nothing to him,* Slatkin concluded. *He probably mangles pedestrians every day.*

"Look out!" shouted a man on the corner. At that, the ferret roused himself. He leaped away, avoiding the horses' iron hooves but knocking down a woman bearing a basket of buns, which spilled over the pavement.

"Sorry, mum," Slatkin hastily apologized. "I weren't watching, I'm afraid." Offering his paw, he tried to help the woman up.

"Look what you done!" the woman cried, pointing to the buns rolling in the gutter. "How am I supposed to sell these now?" She aimed a kick at the ferret, who skipped nimbly over the swinging boot.

"Sell 'em same as you would before, I reckon," Slatkin replied, brushing street grime off one of the rolls. "Unless you wants to charge more for the extra seasoning."

Though he was shaken by the near miss, Slatkin managed to appease the woman and assist her in scooping up her wares. In the process, two buns somehow found their way into the ferret's pocket.

Slatkin trudged through the city traffic until he arrived outside the doctor's rented town house in Renfield Place, Chelsea. He stood on the pavement, leaning against the wrought-iron fence. Panting from the excitement and exertion of the trek, he coughed again and spat. *It's the dampness,* he thought. *Gets into your lungs and pushes out the wind. Why does London have to be so damp, even in June? It's like you was inhaling the Thames with every breath.* He spat once more. *And why is all London buildings so streaked and sooty? Look at these houses here. Gentlemen's homes, yet every one of 'em blackened like a miner's face. If this ain't the dirtiest city in the world, I don't know what is.*

The ferret slumped to the ground. Pulling off his right boot, he examined the worn sole. *And furthermore, why has I got holes in the bottoms of my boots? Don't them advertisements for Norris's Horse-Skin Boots promise that they'll "last well"? Well, they ain't lasted well enough for me, and if I has my way, I'll never steal another pair o' Norris boots again!*

Sometimes Slatkin thought it would be better to move on. London was too much of everything: too big, too loud, too expensive, and too likely to be run by men a hundred times more dishonest than he was. It seemed the city was always looking for a way to flatten him, just as it had demolished the slum rookery where he grew up. Drove the Holborn Viaduct straight through it, they did. Scattered the tenants like bugs. Of course, when he remembered the filth, disease, crime, and misery that had crowded every corner of his childhood home, Slatkin thought he wouldn't have minded knocking it down himself.

And yet, London was the greatest city in the greatest country in the greatest empire in the world. Everyone knew that. And it was his home—the only home the ferret had ever known. He didn't really want to leave it, even had he possessed the money for a ticket, which he certainly did not.

There was one more thing for Slatkin to wonder about as he waited on the sidewalk in Renfield Place: he wondered why he had ever agreed to work for the doctor. He should have told that Toby Thigpen to shove off. Toby was a no-good, swindling pig, and his doctor friend wasn't to be trusted.

Unfortunately, Slatkin owed Toby money. So the ferret had agreed to meet with the doctor in St. James's Park. And the minute he laid eyes on the doctor, Slatkin knew he would regret going along with Toby's plan. The ferret had lived enough, and seen enough, and had enough calamity come crashing down upon his head, to develop certain instincts about people. And those instincts instantly warned him that the doctor was not someone he should do business with.

And yet . . . there was the money. There was always the money. Slatkin had very strong feelings about that, too. And the strongest feeling was that if he didn't go to work for the doctor and pay Toby his money, then Toby would turn him into glue.

Fear tickled the back of Slatkin's neck. He looked up at the narrow windows of the doctor's town house. Was the doctor looking down on him right now with those chilling eyes?

Slatkin was naturally high-strung; that did not make him a coward. Not in this instance, at least. The ferret shook off his misgivings. "Slatkin," he said to himself, "you is not in the bag yet. And with any luck, you never will be." With that he stood up, straightened his scuffed bowler hat, mounted the steps, and rang the bell.

The butler admitted Slatkin to the doctor's home. The butler had a long, thin nose, earlobes that nearly brushed his collar, and an expression that displayed a total lack of trust in the ferret. He stared Slatkin to a halt, then marched slowly up the stairs to the drawing room, leaving the ferret to pace alone in the hallway, his fists jammed into the pockets of his coat.

Not going to kowtow to him nor his snooty butler, Slatkin decided. *I got no reason to scrape. I done all the doctor paid me for. Who coulda done more, I ask? If he ain't happy, he can take his business elsewhere. Didn't pay me to turn the city upside down, did he? Two pounds, he give me. Two pounds don't go so far these days. Not these days, when a bloke won't give you the time o' day for less than half a crown. And that's not to mention expenses. I got expenses to consider.* The ferret swallowed hard. His throat felt thick and dry as a plank. *Got a right to wet my whistle a bit, don't I?*

On one side of the hallway stood a narrow table bearing a silver salver for calling cards. Above the table hung a mirror in a gilt frame. The ferret stopped pacing to regard his image in the mirror.

Slatkin's face was mostly tan, with patches of white around his dark eyes and at the tips of his upright ears. The nose was small and pink, or sometimes red, if he was in especially good spirits. His coat, a check tweed, was worn to a shine at the collar, and the breast pocket flapped loose at one side. The ferret had "pinched" the garment several years earlier at a second-hand clothing market in Petticoat Lane.

"So what if you ain't posh?" Slatkin said, brushing dust from his lapels. "You're an honorable member of a dishonorable profession. That's more than some politicians can say. Besides," he continued, noting the crack in one corner of the mirror, the worn finish on the table, "the doctor ain't so well off as all that. I been in better places than this." He smiled slyly, winking at his reflection. "Of course, I wasn't exactly invited to those places. And the owners was mostly absent at the time."

The ferret lifted the silver platter off the table, examining it closely. "Cheap stuff," he declared. "Might as well eat cheese off it."

At that moment, the butler reappeared at the top of the stairs. "Put that down!" he ordered. Slatkin immediately dropped the salver, which landed on the table with a loud clang.

The butler glared disapprovingly. "Dr. Van Detta will see you now."

Dr. Emil Van Detta sat behind a desk in the drawing room, writing carefully in a notebook. The doctor was forty-five and completely bald, save for a sprig of red hair that dangled above his forehead. His eyebrows were as bushy as his hair was thin, the ends entwining above his nose, which bent to one side and was creased by a scar slicing across the bridge.

Slatkin waited attentively, but the doctor went on writing slowly, clutching the pen in his thick fist. Knowing that he should not speak first, the ferret allowed his gaze to slip around the room.

The drawing room was small and untidy. The clutter consisted mostly of books and papers, which wavered in tall stacks on the desk, chairs, and floor. In addition to the books, there were jars of specimens, wooden carvings of strange creatures, stones with inscriptions in languages the ferret didn't recognize, skulls, masks, clay pots, a stuffed owl, and other odds and ends.

Slatkin's eye was drawn to a paperweight on the desk—a jade carving of a bat-winged gargoyle with sparkling green eyes.

Ugly thing, the ferret thought. *Still, if them eyes is real emeralds, it would fetch a nice price.*

"Casing the place, Slatkin?"

The doctor's question snapped the ferret to attention. "Oh, no, sir," he answered quickly. "Not at all, sir. Just admiring some of your fine art."

"You wouldn't know fine art if Michelangelo himself carved it on your thick skull," the doctor replied.

"You're right about that, sir. No argument there. When it comes to art, I am as ignorant as a ox."

Van Detta continued his writing. Beads of sweat formed between the ferret's eyes. He tugged at his coat buttons.

"Tell me, Slatkin," the doctor said at last, "when we met three weeks ago, did I not deliver certain funds into your hands?"

"You did, sir," the ferret replied. "And you did it most proper."

"And I instructed you to use these funds to acquire certain information, did I not?"

"Right again, sir. You was as clear as glass."

"And have you acquired the information?" the doctor asked.

Slatkin cleared his throat. "Well, sir, now, I have made a very considerable effort—a very considerable and honest effort—to obtain the information you desired. Really I have, sir. But—"

"But what have you found out?"

The ferret started to undo his coat. "It pains me greatly, sir—you being such a fair and decent employer and all—to report that there is not a lot to be found out about the personage you are seeking. He don't seem to be known to a lot of people. Leastwise, not at this time. Leastwise, not to the people I know, and"—the ferret puffed himself up—"old Slatkin, he knows the people what needs to be known in this city. So I'm thinking he must be a very mysterious personage, don't you see? He don't want to be found. Which makes my job of finding him all the more difficult, which is already hard enough in a city of this size, which is filled with people who ain't been found yet, won't never be found, or been found to everyone's lasting disappointment. Not to mention that there are people about who would gladly take a ferret's money in exchange for information that is not worth the paper it were written on, if them scamps could write."

"Is there a point to this?" Van Detta inquired.

"My point is, sir, that I can say quite confidently that the personage you seek may be here in London. More than that, I am not able to say at this time."

The doctor's face was blank. "And you consider this a revelation worth two pounds?" he asked.

"Two pounds don't buy so much information, not these days," Slatkin insisted. "I tried all my sources. I put money in the right hands."

"Yes, you certainly put a good deal of money into the hands of the proprietor of The Jolly Oyster. He supplied you with a copious amount of liquid information, I believe."

Slatkin stared guiltily at the floor, while the doctor resumed his slow writing. Every scratch of the pen point pricked at the ferret's nerves.

Finally, Van Detta set aside his pen. "Do you know what I would like, Slatkin?"

"No, sir," the ferret answered.

"You . . . for stew."

Slatkin dropped his hat, which bounced across the floor.

"But I shall have to let that pass for now," the doctor continued. "I have more pressing business. To complete it, I may yet require your inept assistance."

"Yes, sir. Anything you wish, sir," the ferret piped, as he recovered his bowler. "I'm ready to try again. And this time, sir, if I knew a bit more about this personage you are seeking? This Barksdale?"

Van Detta closed his book. "What I previously knew of Barksdale, I knew mostly from genealogies and local records," he explained, sweeping his arm over the clutter on his desk. "While you were draining your glass at the public house, I was studying documents in the Round Room at the Record Office. My work requires a great deal of research, sir. I assure you, it is not a profession for the lazy or half-witted."

"I can see you is as whole-witted as they come, sir," Slatkin remarked.

Clearing his throat, the doctor went on. "It was while I was at the Record Office that I had a stroke of luck. I met a clerk who claimed to have seen Mr. Barksdale briefly several years ago. He gave me some vital information. As I told you previously, Mr. Barksdale is a hound."

"Right, sir. A gentleman of the canine persuasion. So you said."

"I believe he has a substantial income," the doctor continued.

"As luck would have it, I have no prejudice against money, sir," Slatkin stated, "especially when it has found its way into my own pocket." The wink he gave was not returned by the doctor.

"I am told that he is frequently accompanied by a servant," Van Detta went on. "A bobtailed rat named Potts."

"Another stroke of luck!" the ferret exclaimed. "I come from a long line of rat-catchers. My grandfather was once invited to chase rats at Buckingham Palace."

"Yes, I can see you come from one of England's best families," said the doctor scornfully. "There is one more thing about Barksdale that you should perhaps know. It is a fact that was hidden from the clerk, as it has been hidden from all but a few people in England. It is also the reason for my sojourn in London. Can you guess what that fact is, ferret?"

Slatkin shook his head.

Van Detta lowered his voice. "Barksdale is a vampire."

Oh, blimey, thought the ferret, *do I need any more reasons to run from this job?* He sucked in his lips and cocked his head to one side. "A vampire, sir?" he said uncertainly.

"To be precise, he is a *Canis vesperinus*—a vampire hound."

"I didn't know I was hunting for no vampire," said Slatkin, scratching his nose.

"You should feel honored, ferret," the doctor asserted. "Vampire hunting is among the oldest and noblest of professions. Society, however, does not always appreciate our efforts," he added sourly. Rising from his chair, Van Detta came out from behind the desk. He loomed above the ferret, hands behind his back, his broad chest testing the limits of his blue waistcoat.

"Vampires are an abomination," the doctor stated, as if he were lecturing in a classroom. "They are evil, a plague upon mankind. Therefore, for the good of humanity, they must be eliminated. It is this burden which I have taken upon myself. I have tracked these monsters through the rain forests of Brazil. I have pursued them across the Russian steppes. Have you ever heard of the mouse vampire of Minsk?"

"A mouse vampire, sir?" said Slatkin.

"A vicious beast, with fangs as long as your thumb. It took me six months to trap him. Six months of bitter Russian nights. Shivering! Starving! I was forced to eat my mittens! Can you imagine it?"

"I once tried to eat a butcher's apron," said the ferret, sticking out his tongue. "It weren't a success."

"But of course you haven't heard of the mouse vampire," snapped Van Detta, throwing up his hands. "The newspapers refuse to tell my story! Everyone knows of this English detective, this Sherlock Holmes! But the world knows nothing of me! What must a man do to get his name in the papers?"

"In my experience, it helps if you get arrested," Slatkin suggested.

The doctor glowered at the ferret. "Sometimes I wonder why I ever took up this profession," he grumbled.

"Sometimes I wonder the same thing about myself," Slatkin remarked. "But as soon as my stomach starts growling, I remember why I do what I do."

"And right now your job is to assist me in tracking down the vampire hound," Van Detta reminded him. "Do you think you might manage that?"

"If you don't mind my suggesting it, sir, wouldn't it be easier to lay an accusation against this Barksdale? Let Scotland Yard track him down?"

"No," said the doctor. "I find that the authorities do not take my work seriously. I will not be mocked by fat policemen. Therefore, I must pluck this nightbird myself."

"Well, sir, if we don't find this vampire hound, I'm sure there are plenty of other bloodsuckers in this city for you to tackle—my landlord, for instance."

With a sudden, powerful movement, Van Detta grabbed Slatkin by the throat, lifting him off the floor. "This is no joking matter, ferret," the doctor hissed, his red face inches from Slatkin's nose. "This is my life's work. If I am not rewarded, you are not rewarded. Do you understand?"

"Yes, sir," the ferret squeaked. The doctor's grip was like a noose around his neck.

"The next time you report to me, you will have something worth reporting."

Slatkin nodded. Van Detta lowered the ferret to the floor and released his grip.

"You won't regret giving me another chance, sir," Slatkin promised, rubbing his neck.

"I regret everything about you," the doctor replied. "Now, go away."

Turning quickly on his heel, the ferret marched out of the drawing room and down the stairs. He gave the butler one final scowl before hopping down the front steps to the street.

Vampires, Slatkin thought, as he picked his way through the afternoon traffic. *Who in his right mind goes looking for vampires? Ought to lock that doctor in Bedlam with the other lunatics. Ought to lock me up for ever talking to him. Vampires and madmen—with the likes o' them running around loose, a bloke would be safer in prison.* He kicked at an orange peel lying on the sidewalk. *But I been hired, I guess. And that doctor don't seem a man who takes kindly to being disappointed.*

The ferret licked his lips. *I know one thing: vampire-finding is bound to be thirsty work. I better find some bloke in The Jolly Oyster who will stand me a drink.*

II

On the Prowl

Late-Victorian London was famous for many things; one of them was fog. Night mists floated off the River Thames; "stinks" rose from the glue, paint, and bleach factories of Southwark; together they mingled with smoke from the thousands of coal and gas fires that warmed, lit, fed, and drove the great city, forming a noxious cloud that poured over the streets like dirty cream.

It was very late on a foggy night in June. A pair of figures made their way down Oxford Street. Barksdale's boots thumped energetically on the pavement, his cane rapping the stones with every stride. Darkness and fog were no hindrance to the hound; thanks to his vampire ancestors, he possessed a night vision that pierced the gloom like the beam of a lighthouse. The same could not be said for his companion—a plump little rat, scurrying to keep up with his master on legs that were nearly as stubby as his tail, all the while darting and weaving to avoid the carts, posts, barrels, cabs, pedestrians, and horses that loomed suddenly out of the fog.

"It's just that I wouldn't blame you if you did complain, Potts," Barksdale was saying. "These nocturnal excursions of mine must be terribly wearisome for you. They are wearisome for me, I assure you."

"I really don't mind, sir," Tilney Potts replied, puffing. "I have always enjoyed a brisk walk. My Aunt Dora says that a walk in the night air is good for the digestion. Of course, the dampness is bad for her rheumatism, so she herself never goes out after sunset."

"Well, I have neither bad digestion nor rheumatism," Barksdale stated. "But I do have vampire blood in my veins, and that blood seems to demand that I prowl the night, when I would much prefer to be home in bed."

"I know what you mean, sir. I had a bit of insomnia myself, when I was younger."

"Was it bothersome, Potts?"

"Oh, no, sir. Fortunately, I slept right through it."

The hound laughed. "Potts, you should be performing in music halls. But I'm not about to let you go."

"Perhaps you should try my Aunt Dora's remedy for sleeplessness," Tilney suggested. "You boil chamomile and crumbs of brown bread in white wine vinegar. Then you spread the mixture on a cloth and bind the cloth to the soles of your feet."

"Thank you, Potts," Barksdale replied, "but it is not my feet that I wish to put to sleep. And a glass of warm milk would do just as well, I suppose."

"I'm sure you are right, sir. To be honest, I doubt that Aunt Dora has ever needed her own remedy. She has more talent for napping than any creature I ever saw. She has been known to doze off in the middle of pouring tea. It has led to some soggy tea cakes, sir, I assure you. Not to mention a few soggy laps."

"I thought I was well acquainted with all the branches of your enormous family," said the hound, "but Aunt Dora is new to me."

Tilney Potts hurdled the outstretched legs of a scruffy man who, having become too familiar with a nearby gin establishment, was now sitting propped against a lamppost, his jaw hanging slack upon his chest.

"Just a moment, Potts," said Barksdale. "This fellow could do with some assistance."

Leaning down, the hound placed his gloved paws under the man's arms and lifted him easily to his feet. The man's eyes wobbled, then seemed to focus with terror on the visage of the hound.

"Don't be alarmed, friend," Barksdale said soothingly. "You've had rather a long night, so we're going to make you a bit more comfortable. Potts, is that a coffee shop just ahead?"

"It is, indeed, sir," Potts replied, rushing to get the door.

Barksdale maneuvered the man inside the shop, where he placed him on a chair. Tilney stationed himself beside the chair, leaning against the man to prevent his toppling onto the floor.

The hound removed his hat and addressed the proprietor, a small, bug-eyed man, whose shirt and apron were decorated with matching stains.

"Sir, this is a grand moment for your humble establishment," Barksdale announced. "For I am pleased to bring you a most illustrious patron"—he indicated the man sprawled on the chair—"His Lordship, the Earl of Dimwitty."

The "earl's" head tipped over the back of the chair, and he began snoring loudly.

The proprietor raised his eyebrows. "That beggar? An earl?" he exclaimed, leaning across the long counter. "If he's an earl, then I'm the Queen o' Sheba!" The little man laughed loudly, delighted by his own wit.

"Then I am pleased to meet Your Majesty," Barksdale replied, with a deep bow. "What luck to find two highborn persons in such a low place."

The proprietor abruptly stopped laughing. "I run a business here," he said, "not a home for derelicts."

Barksdale stepped forward and placed a shilling on the counter. "Then I trust you will make it your business to look after this man until he awakes, at which time I would like you to fill him full of black coffee and feed him breakfast. Is that agreeable to Your Majesty?"

The proprietor frowned at the sleeping man, then at the hound. He slipped the coin off the counter and into his pocket. "I suppose it's all right," he said grudgingly.

"Very good," Barksdale replied, with a smile that revealed two oversize canine teeth. "I knew I could count on your generosity." Taking up his hat and cane, the hound bowed to the proprietor. "I hope Your Majesty will have a pleasant evening," he said.

"Pleasant evening," chimed Tilney, tipping his bowler. Then he followed his master out the door.

Back on the street, the rat asked, "Do you really believe he will comply with your wishes, sir?"

"I believe so, Potts," said Barksdale. "Most men will do what they have been paid to do. The proprietor may not be as generous with the coffee and bacon as we would hope, but that poor fellow will have a better breakfast than he could get lying in the gutter."

The hound then returned to the previous topic of conversation. "Tell me more of your Aunt Dora," he said.

"She is my aunt by reason of her marriage to my Uncle Josiah, the fourteenth of my father's brothers," Tilney explained. "They currently reside in Willesden. Dora is a sweet old rat, though she does have her odd moments. She once chased Uncle Josiah all the way to Mayfair with a hot pudding. We still don't know what she had in mind, sir."

Barksdale chuckled. "Potts, your family is as colorful as it is large."

"I cannot dispute its size, sir," Tilney responded. "My first cousins alone could form two regiments."

"It's a good thing to have a large family," Barksdale observed.

"Except, perhaps, at dinnertime," Tilney countered.

"I see your point, Potts. Still, I think it is better to have relatives about. Since my mother's passing, I have had no family of my own. I suppose I am an orphan, Potts. Can someone nearing forty be an orphan?"

"I don't see why not, sir."

"Then I am an orphan, adrift in the cold, cruel world," Barksdale said in a melodramatic tone. "If only Mr. Dickens were alive; he could make a novel of me."

The hound's prowl continued—through Soho, where the foreigners congregated, past the Royal Opera House in Covent Garden, along the Strand, then over Fleet Street, vibrating with the roar of printing presses. Master and servant had just turned toward the river, the thick mist wafting in their faces, when Barksdale suddenly thrust his cane across Tilney's path.

"What is it, sir?" the rat whispered.

The hound placed a finger to his lips. Through the fog, he had witnessed two figures forcing a third into an alley up ahead.

Barksdale crept closer, Tilney Potts at his side. The hound could now see the figures clearly, though Tilney was not yet able to make them out. Then a match was struck and a candle lit, dimly illuminating two ferrets accosting a young woman.

"We wants the money, dearie," said one of the ferrets. He was stoop-shouldered and had to tilt his head back to address the woman, whose elbows were grasped tightly by the other ferret.

"I ain't got it," the woman protested.

"Oh, you got it," the ferret replied. "You got it right there in your purse. And you better give it over, before I breaks your pretty little head."

"He'll do it," the second ferret warned.

The woman began to cry. "I can't give it up," she whimpered. "I need the money to feed my babes. Please, sir, I beg you. Have pity on my children."

The first ferret stepped away from the woman. With a short, sharp bark of exasperation, he yanked his hat from his head and slapped it on his thigh.

"Why does they always have to start bawling?" the ferret complained. "Do they all know that old Slatkin has the softest heart in London? Is it writ on my face? How is a bloke with my sensitive nature to earn a living, when women is all the time gushing like this?"

"You is too kind for your own good," remarked his partner, whose name was Grimshaw. "Perhaps I could break her head?"

At this, the woman began to cry all the more.

Barksdale had seen and heard enough. He turned to his servant. "Stay here," he whispered. "I will deal with them."

Barksdale was not a full-blooded vampire hound. His mother, Anna, had not been infected with the curse. Barksdale, therefore, was not able to change his shape, in the manner of most vampires. Still, though he could not assume the form of a bat, he could climb and cling like one. Placing his cane between his teeth, the hound went swiftly up the bricks of the building that formed one side of the alley. In moments, he had disappeared into the fog.

Slatkin spoke to the woman again. "All right, dearie, this is your last warning. If you don't give us what we want, my partner here, who is clearly a brute, will bash you over the head and take it."

The woman stopped crying. "Then I expect you better try it," she said fiercely, "'cause I worked hard for this money, and I ain't giving it up to the likes of you."

"All right," said Grimshaw. "If you wants it rough, then rough it will be." Turning the woman loose, he drew a club from inside his coat.

Slatkin laid a paw on his partner's arm. "Let's not be hasty," he whispered. "We has her scared. She may give it up yet."

"And I may win the Derby," muttered Grimshaw. "What you waiting for? Are we doing this job or not?"

"We're doing it," said Slatkin. "We just ain't doing it hasty, all right? Maybe if we brings Chuggers into the mix . . . "

While the ferrets debated, Barksdale nimbly traversed the side of the building and seated himself on a ledge ten feet above the alley floor. Now his voice boomed out of the fog. "Gentlemen, I advise you to leave off bothering this woman and be on your way."

"Hey! Who's that?" cried Slatkin, whirling around.

"Go," Barksdale ordered. "Now!"

"Get the money!" Slatkin shouted. His partner grabbed for the woman's purse, but the woman resisted doggedly. Holding fast to the purse with her left hand, she used her right to twist the club from Grimshaw's grasp. She began to beat the ferret with his own weapon.

"Ow! Gimme some help, will ya?!" Grimshaw howled, as the blows fell on his head and neck.

Before Slatkin could take a step, however, he found his way barred by the tall, slender figure of the vampire hound.

"Let the woman go," Barksdale repeated, tapping his cane upon the palm of his glove.

Slatkin was so astonished by the sudden appearance of the hound that, for a few moments, he could not say or do anything. When he finally recovered, he gave a harsh cry:

"CHUGGERS!"

Back at the entrance to the alley, Tilney Potts was straining his eyes to follow the action. Suddenly, a bulky form, huffing like a steam engine, charged past him and attacked his master from the rear. The two ferrets immediately forgot about the woman and joined in the assault on Barksdale, kicking and swinging at the hound as he struggled to free himself from the third hoodlum.

"Mr. Barksdale! Come away, sir!" Tilney shouted. But the largest attacker—it now appeared to be a bear—had the hound locked in his burly arms.

Tilney did not hesitate. Reaching into his coat, he drew out his own "life preserver," a short wooden club he always carried when he went out at night. With a yell, the little rat rushed down the alley, leaped onto the bear's back, and began whacking him on the head. Startled, the bear released Barksdale. Then, roaring with anger, the bear reached over his shoulder, grabbed the rat by his coat, and flung him into the air.

"Potts!" cried Barksdale.

Tilney felt himself whirling through the night. There was a sharp pain in his right shoulder, and then blackness.

III

Tilney's Pain

Harker Lane was little more than an alley pinched between a druggist on one side and a tailor's shop on the other. The foot and carriage trade pushing busily along Oxford Street never gave it a first glance, let alone a second. It went unnoticed by the wandering knife grinders and furniture menders, the flower girls and porters, and the costers with their donkey carts full of fruits and vegetables. Even the orderly boys in their uniform jackets and caps, daring to scramble in and out of traffic to sweep up the never-ending supply of horse droppings—even they failed to mark Harker Place on their mental map of London. Only the dustmen who came to empty the waste bins seemed to be aware of its existence. And even they never ventured to the far end of the alley. Had curiosity or duty ever led them to such a point, they would have discovered a high brick wall covered with ivy. In the middle of the wall, hidden behind the green, leafy tapestry, was a low iron door, securely locked. Beyond the door, the alley widened into a small courtyard, containing some dog roses and a stunted but tenacious oak tree. A gravel walk led to a tall stuccoed town house, which had been tucked behind Oxford Street some sixty years earlier by a prosperous soap manufacturer who valued his privacy. In the Royal Blue Book it was listed as the home of one "Jonathan Kennelworthy, Esquire." But in fact, this secluded home, whose official address was 1 Harker Lane, had for the past twelve years been the residence of Mr. Barksdale— gentleman, philanthropist, and vampire hound.

Tilney Potts's room was at the back of the second floor. The curtains had been drawn, but light leaked around them, so the rat knew it must be day. He was lying on his back, with the bedclothes tucked up to his chin. His right eye felt swollen, but it pained him less than his right shoulder, which throbbed like a kettledrum. His back was stiff from lying in the same position for many hours. When he attempted to roll over, however, his injured shoulder pounded even more sharply, and he was forced to sink back on the pillow.

To escape the pain, Tilney tried to direct his mind to happier things. He pictured himself as a child, skating on the frozen Thames with his brothers and sisters. His sister Nan—older by four years and his favorite sibling—was skating beside him, holding his hand. They were skating fast, their laughter curling in the air behind them. Tilney let go his sister's hand. He glided through a pack of children, friends he had barely thought of for many years. He leaned into a sweeping turn. His skates slid out from under him. He fell and slipped away on the ice. It was not a hard fall. When his sister reached him, he was still laughing. And yet, his shoulder ached. Why did it ache so, from such a little bump? He hoped he would not need a doctor; his parents could not afford it. He saw his mother and father at the table with their meager hoard of coins. Their faces were pinched with worry. "Don't count them!" Tilney begged. "You'll only know how poor we are!"

And then, suddenly, the scene shifted. Now it was summer. The river wound through muddy banks. Tilney was standing on the pier near Billingsgate. His father stood beside him. Pointing to the colliers moored in the river, his father said, "Soon you'll be old enough to join us there, Tilney. It's hard work, unloading coal. But you'll take to it, like your brothers." Tilney turned away from his father. He began to run. His father called after him.

"Potts? Potts, are you awake?"

Tilney blinked his large brown eyes. There was a moment's confusion, before he sensed the familiar surroundings—the chair and the dressing table, the prints of sailing ships on the walls. Turning his head toward the door, he answered hoarsely, "Come in, sir."

The door opened slowly and Barksdale entered, bearing a tea service on a tray, which he placed carefully on the small table beside Tilney's bed. "Were you asleep?" asked the hound.

"I suppose I was, sir," Tilney said. "Though I didn't know it until I awoke."

"You've been resting for quite a while. Would you like me to open the curtains?"

"That would be fine, sir, as long as . . . "

"You needn't worry about me," Barksdale assured him. "Thanks to my mother, I can stand four or five hours of direct sunlight without suffering any harm." He pulled back the drapes. Tilney's good eye squinted at the light. The hound drew the upholstered chair beside the bed and sat down.

Barksdale's eyes were a soft blue-gray, like the shadows on the clouds at sunset. At that moment, they were filled with concern for his servant. "How are you feeling?" he asked.

"Not so bad, sir. My head is a bit fuzzy. And my shoulder aches a little. But not too much, really."

"Your right eye has been blackened," said Barksdale. "Can you see out of it?"

Tilney shut his left eye. "Yes, sir, I can see. It is a bit cloudy, but I can see. But how are you, sir? Were you badly injured? It was a desperate struggle, what I saw of it."

"I am well," Barksdale answered, gently rubbing a tender spot on his ribs. "A few bumps. Nothing to bother about."

"And the woman?" Tilney asked.

"She escaped shortly after you launched your assault."

"I'm glad of that," Tilney said. "It was a terrible blunder, sir. I should have done as you told me. I should have stayed where I was. Instead, I gave you something else to worry about, when you were already beset on every side. I'm very sorry, sir."

"On the contrary, Potts," Barksdale replied. "Your attack caught my assailants completely by surprise. While they were distracted, I was able to break free, then hit them again, before they were able to recover. After that, they wished only to get away as quickly as possible. Furthermore, it is I who should apologize to you. It was my need to prowl that placed you in such danger in the first place. This cursed vampire blood . . ." His voice trailed off.

Tilney gave his master a look of sympathy. "It is not your fault that you were born with such a past, sir."

The hound gazed at his paws, folded on his lap. His claws were quickly growing long again, another legacy from his vampire father; he would have to file them down. "No, I suppose it cannot be helped," he said.

"And as my Uncle Nathan always says," Tilney offered, "'What cannot be helped cannot be faulted.'"

Barksdale nodded slightly. Without raising his eyes, he asked, "Have you never wished to be something different, Potts?"

"Of course I have, sir," was the rat's immediate reply. "I wished it often when I was young. I wish it sometimes even now, if you'll pardon my saying it, sir. I venture even Her Majesty makes that wish from time to time—though I don't really presume to know what Her Majesty might think. And I believe I got my wish, sir, for I am different. My present life is not the life that was set down for me at birth, sir. It is not the life my mother and father imagined for me. And I won't say they have not been a bit disappointed in that regard—my father, in particular. But it is a good life, sir. And if I have to lead that life with some small regrets and a stubby tail, then I ought not complain, for fate has been less kind to many others. Take my cousin Ezra, born with an extra nose."

"An extra nose?" said Barksdale.

"An extra nose, sir. Poor Ezra. As you can imagine, it is terribly difficult to speak with him face-to-face; you are always going cross-eyed with looking at both noses at once. And when he gets the sniffles, sir—well, you don't want to think about it."

Barksdale smiled. "You have a way with a story, Potts."

Tilney blushed. "I'm afraid I talk too much, sir," he said.

"Would you like some tea?" the hound asked.

Tilney hesitated. "I don't wish to sound ungrateful, sir, but it is not right for you to serve me in this way."

"Don't talk nonsense, Potts," said Barksdale. "Kindness is always correct." He poured out two cups from the pot on the tray. "Now, can you sit up?"

"Perhaps. If you could help," Tilney replied.

Barksdale placed an arm behind the rat's shoulders and raised him slowly. With the other paw, he slid a pillow behind Tilney's back.

"Thank you, sir. That's much better."

Tilney smiled bravely, but it was obvious to Barksdale that his servant was in pain. "I blame myself," he fumed. "I should have routed those ruffians on my own . . . even if it meant using the bite."

"Oh, no, sir!" Tilney exclaimed. "Not the bite. Not on my account. Not on anyone's account. You know the evil it can do, sir. You promised your mother that you would never use it."

"Yes. And on no account should a son break a promise to his mother. Isn't that right, Potts?" Barksdale observed ruefully.

"I'm sure you would regret it, sir."

The hound handed Tilney his cup and saucer. Master and servant sipped their tea for a time in silence.

"I've had the surgeon here to look at your shoulder," Barksdale related. "He says it is badly bruised, but, fortunately, nothing is broken. I am to rub some Elliman's Embrocation on it later. That should fix you up."

"I do appreciate it, sir," Tilney replied. "But are you certain it was wise to send for the surgeon?"

"Dr. Mullbender is a trustworthy gentleman," Barksdale assured him. "He was most highly recommended by my solicitor, Mr. Church. He will not give us away. But you are right to advise caution, Potts. We have good reason to be discreet. Even more than usual."

Barksdale retrieved a folded section of *The Times* off the tea tray and handed it to the rat. "First column, near the bottom," he instructed.

Tilney scanned down the newspaper page until a particular item in bold print caught his eye:

BARKSDALE, YOUR TIME HAS COME.
E. V. D., 22 Renfield Place, Chelsea

Tilney lowered the paper. "'E.V.D.' Is this the gentleman we have heard about, sir? The vampire hunter?"

"Yes. It appears Dr. Van Detta has come to London."

"He threatens you, sir. Perhaps you should inform Scotland Yard."

"No, Potts. It would not do for Scotland Yard to open a file on me. Besides, I believe this notice is more of a challenge than a threat. That's why he has included his address. He's hoping I will pay him a visit."

"And will you, sir?" asked Tilney, with a worried look.

Barksdale gazed evenly at his servant, but his ears twitched with interest. "Who knows, Potts? May I pour you some more tea?"

IV

Chuggers

While Barksdale and Potts conversed in the quiet of Tilney's room, a related discussion was taking place amid the midday clamor in The Jolly Oyster.

Slatkin reached for his pint with his right arm, grimaced, and switched to his left. "Nearly took my arm off, he did, that hound," the ferret complained to his companion. "And didn't he crack Grimshaw a good one across the snout? Then give him the boot in the tail? The way Grim' took off, I'll wager he run halfway to Dover."

"I knowed that Grimshaw were no good in a scrape," said Chuggers the bear.

Slatkin bristled. "And what about you?" he charged. "Why didn't you pitch in sooner? You was supposed to be watching our backs. What was you, catching forty winks? Larking about? I bet you was larking about, 'stead of watching our backs."

"I weren't larking," said Chuggers, staring sullenly at the ferret with his good eye. The bear had only one good eye (the right) and one good ear (the left). His other ear had been mangled in a childhood fight with a mastiff; his other eye, now covered by a patch, had been lost to an illness, which had also caused portions of his fur to fall out. The result was a face no one would rescue from a rubbish heap.

"Well, you certainly took your time," Slatkin grumbled. "If it weren't larking, I don't know what it was." With his left paw, he gingerly examined the tip of his nose. "Caught me one with that cane of his," he said.

"Think you is the only one what is battered?" Chuggers countered. He pulled off his cloth cap and leaned forward, pointing to the top of his head. "That little rat played my knob like a gong. Feel them lumps on my head. Feel 'em! It's like my head was full of rocks."

"Your head *is* full of rocks," said Slatkin.

"And I weren't larking!" growled Chuggers. He slammed his hefty paw down on the table, rattling their drinks. The din of conversation in the pub ceased momentarily, as all heads turned to the ferret and his companion. When the bear's words were not immediately followed by blows, the other customers went back to their own pursuits.

"All right, all right, you wasn't larking," Slatkin conceded. "It ain't nothing to spill drinks over."

Chuggers pulled his cap low on his forehead and sipped his drink, pouting.

Slatkin pretended to look out the window of the pub, all the while regarding the bear out of the corner of his eye. Like most bears, Chuggers did not own a coat, and his paisley waistcoat had obviously been made for someone else; the buttons and the buttonholes, separated by the bear's girth, remained completely unaware of each other, like villagers living on opposite sides of a mountain. He had no stays, his patched trousers being held up by a length of grimy rope belted around his waist. *He's a walking ragbag,* thought the ferret, shaking his head. Still, Chuggers was good at breaking down doors or lifting up windows. And he could be a devil in a fight . . . assuming he arrived in time.

"Leastwise, now I know for certain that hound is here in London," Slatkin stated.

"What hound?" said his companion.

"The hound I has been searching for this past month," Slatkin replied. "The hound we had our little set-to with last night. The hound that whacked me on the nose."

"Why would you go looking for a hound to whack you on the nose?" asked Chuggers, with a confused expression. "If it's a whack on the nose you wanted, I'd've gladly done it for you."

"No doubt," Slatkin said. "But I weren't looking for him to whack me. I were looking for him to find him. Which I did, in a manner of speaking."

Slatkin proceeded to tell Chuggers—very slowly, with frequent interruptions and repetitions and much rolling of the eyes—how he had been hired by Dr. Van Detta to find the hound.

"And you heard him call the little rat 'Potts,'" Slatkin recounted. "Which can only be that stump-tailed servant of his."

"Which put these lumps on my head," said Chuggers.

"I'm about to add some lumps of my own," Slatkin replied testily, and the bear leaned far back in his chair.

Chuggers said, "Slatkin, you is just like a sort of detective in this case. You is just like that Mr. Sure Luck Holmes."

The ferret cocked his head on one side, then the other, as if to let the comparison roll around in his brain. "I guess you're right, Chuggers," he said, with obvious pleasure. "I am a short, furry Sherlock Holmes. I am the poor man's Sherlock Holmes, most emphasis being on the word 'poor.'"

"So I must be your partner, just as Mr. Holmes has Dr. What-sis," the bear suggested.

Slatkin frowned. "You ain't no doctor," he said. "And what I need a partner for? Ain't I already found the hound?"

"Found him and lost him," Chuggers reminded him. "No

telling how hard it might be to find him again. And suppose you do find him? There might be fisticuffs. What then?"

The ferret drummed his paw on the table.

"Besides," Chuggers continued, his face sagging, "I thought we was friends."

Slatkin looked at the bear, who was doing his best to appear friendless and pitiable, though his actual expression bore a strong resemblance to a sick codfish.

The ferret sighed. "I suppose your brawn might come in handy yet," he said. "Even though you is prone to lark—"

Chuggers shoved his furry fist under Slatkin's nose. "Don't even say it," he warned.

The ferret pursed his lips but said no more. They finished their drinks.

"Now," Chuggers resumed, folding his paws on the table in a businesslike manner, "where is my share?"

"Your share of what?" Slatkin replied.

"My share of what you has been paid to find this hound."

The ferret cast his eyes toward the ceiling. "I knew it! I knew it!" he sputtered. "I knew I would regret this. Why should I give you money, when I have done all the detecting so far by myself?"

"Then how'd I get them lumps on my head?" Chuggers replied indignantly. "And you said we was partners."

"I thought we was friends," Slatkin countered.

"A friend wouldn't hold out on a friend," Chuggers argued.

"With a friend like you, I shall soon be making new friends in the poorhouse!" barked Slatkin.

"I paid for the drinks," Chuggers reminded him. "All I wants now is my half."

Angrily, the ferret dug into his pocket, fished out a coin, and slapped it on the table.

The bear took the coin in his paw. "Tuppence is all?" he said.

"Tuppence is all," Slatkin echoed, "and even that didn't come from the doctor."

"Where'd you get it, then?"

"A distinguished gentleman give it to me in Chancery Lane this morning. I brushed some dirt off his coat."

"How'd his coat get dirty?" Chuggers inquired.

Slatkin winked at the bear. "Someone might've thrown dust on him when he weren't looking, I suppose. The streets is full of that sort of riffraff."

"Sounds like the same sort of a shifty bloke who might try to cheat his partner," Chuggers said. "Are you sure that's all you got in your pocket?" He eyed the ferret suspiciously.

"Unless you wants half a stale bun left over from my breakfast."

Chuggers considered this carefully. "How stale is it?" he asked.

Grinding his teeth, Slatkin stared at the bear. Then he snatched the half-eaten bun from his pocket and threw it on the table. "There! Now you has it all!" he snapped.

Chuggers picked up the scrap and sniffed it. "You is a true friend, giving me your last crumb like that," he said. "I will eat it in honor of our partnership." He tossed the morsel into his mouth and started chewing slowly.

Slatkin pushed himself up from the table. "Come on, partner," he said sourly. "We got to make a report."

V

The Ferret's Tale

·

Slatkin charged through the pigeons in Trafalgar Square like a battleship plowing through heavy seas. Suddenly, he turned on his companion.

"I knew you was a mistake!" the ferret exclaimed. "You been detecting for five minutes, and already you has nearly got us arrested. Why was you bothering that old rat back there?"

"You said we was to keep an eye out for a hound and a no-tail rat, didn't you?" Chuggers replied. "Well, how am I to tell if a rat has no tail, unless I lifts up his coattails?"

"So, was you planning to lift up the coattails of every rat in London, then?" Slatkin snapped.

Chuggers shrugged and brushed away a pigeon that was attempting to light on his head.

"You was lucky that rat didn't set the bobbies on us."

"Don't seem so lucky to me," the bear grumbled, rubbing his sore arm. "That old rat was tough. I never knowed this detecting was such a bruising business."

Chuggers was careful to walk behind Slatkin for a while, and by the time they reached Brompton Road, the ferret's anger had cooled. There they halted to watch shoppers passing in and out of Harrod's department store. They scanned the store windows crammed with flowers, perfumes, silks, stationery, toys and games, shirts and stockings, ribbons and laces, and all types of marvelous goods, pausing longest before a display of cooked partridge and venison.

"What do that say?" asked Chuggers, pointing to a sign with handsome gold lettering.

"'Harrod's Serves the World,'" Slatkin read.

"The whole world?" asked Chuggers.

"I suppose," Slatkin replied. "Provided you has the cash."

The ferret and the bear resumed their walk, but at a slower pace. They gaped at other windows offering goods they could not afford.

"Remember when that mob from the docks looted them shops in Piccadilly?" Slatkin recalled.

"How long ago now?" said Chuggers. "Seven, eight years, I reckon. Quite an uproar, that was."

"Do any looting yourself?" Slatkin asked.

Chuggers shook his head. "Too cold," he said. "I weren't about to traipse across London in midwinter just so some peeler could knock me on the head for stealing a handkerchief. How about you?"

"I don't hold with rioting," said Slatkin, making a face. "Rioting is for amateurs. Anyone can throw a brick through a window."

Turning into Renfield Place, they found Dr. Van Detta coming out of his house, a canvas bag slung over his shoulder.

"What do you want?" asked the doctor, addressing the ferret but casting a critical eye toward the bear.

"Important news, sir," said Slatkin. "We have proof that Barksdale is here in London."

"What proof?"

"Proof as seeing him with our own eyes," the ferret reported. "My partner and me—"

"We is also friends," Chuggers interjected.

"—came to blows with Barksdale and his servant last night."

"How do you know it was Barksdale?" the doctor asked.

"We heard him called by name, sir," said Slatkin. "And the little rat, too."

"What put these lumps on my head," added Chuggers, doffing his cap.

"They will undoubtedly increase your intelligence," Van Detta remarked to the bear.

"Do you really think so, sir?" replied Chuggers, with surprise.

"Almost anything would," said the doctor. "Where did this skirmish occur?"

"In an alley near Blackfriars Bridge," Slatkin told him.

"Were either of you bitten by the hound?" Van Detta asked, looking warily from the ferret to the bear.

Slatkin shook his head. "He showed some terrible fearsome teeth, sir. But he never got them into us."

"You were fortunate. But tell me, how did this encounter come about?"

"Chuggers and me was just walking along like," Slatkin recounted. "Just out for an evening's stroll, up to no harm. All of a sudden, from out of the fog, this vicious hound leaps upon us. Oh, it were a fearsome struggle, sir. But that hound don't know what it is to tangle with a ferret." Slatkin jabbed the air with his fists. "I gave him a few quick blows to the body, then a roundhouse to the chin. He run off like a whipped puppy, sir."

"Did he?" said Van Detta, raising an eyebrow. "And is that how you remember the event, Mr. . . . Chuggers, is it?"

Chuggers blinked his good eye at the doctor, then turned toward the ferret. "It were mostly like that," he answered slowly. He squinted at Slatkin, who looked away. "Except maybe I give and got more blows than some might care to remember."

Dr. Van Detta nodded. "This cowardly attack, this ambush in the darkness, is quite typical of these monsters," he said. "Something similar happened to me in Jamaica several years ago. I was hunting alone one night, when suddenly something swooped down from a tall tree and struck me on the head."

"Were it a vampire bat?" asked Slatkin, wide-eyed.

"Well, no, actually," the doctor replied. "It was a coconut. But I assure you, sir—when I regained consciousness, I gave it a good thrashing."

"Which were well-deserved," Slatkin added.

"I once dropped a sack of apples on my foot," Chuggers offered. "Just to show 'em who was boss, I ate ever' one."

"I am a bit surprised that you were able to drive the hound away so easily," Van Detta resumed. "His powers must be weaker than I surmised. Still, we must not underestimate him. Treachery and cunning, hatred of all things living and decent—these are the hallmarks of the race. Neither time nor breeding can ever alter that. That is why extermination is our only recourse."

The coldness with which this judgment was pronounced raised the hair on Slatkin's neck.

"And after you routed the hound, did you follow him to his lair?" the doctor inquired.

"I regret to say he lost us in the fog, sir," Slatkin replied.

"So we still have no idea where he resides?"

"Not yet, sir. But me and Chuggers are on the case, sir," said the ferret. "Now that we knows the hound is here in London, it's only a matter of time before we discovers his hideout."

Van Detta looked from Slatkin to Chuggers and back again. He sniffed. "There will, of course, be no additional outlay of cash for Mr. Chuggers," he pronounced. "Is that understood?"

"Oh, yes, sir. That's quite clear," Slatkin answered. "Chuggers and me, we will split anything and everything that's paid to me. We is friends, you see."

"And partners," added Chuggers.

The doctor removed his hat. His lock of red hair twisted across his scalp like a protruding vein. Drawing a handkerchief from his pocket, he wiped his brow. "We have sun today," he stated. "In my profession, a sunny day is a good day for hunting." He slipped the canvas bag from his shoulder and handed it to the ferret. "You may carry this. Come along." He began to march away down the street.

Slatkin turned to his partner. "You may carry this," he said, handing the bag to the bear. "Come along." Quickly, he followed Dr. Van Detta.

Chuggers paused, looked around, then slipped the bag on his shoulder and hurried to catch up with the others.

VI

Vampire Hunting

With Dr. Van Detta setting a brisk pace, the trio proceeded back up Brompton Road, across Knightsbridge, and into Hyde Park.

The fine weather had brought more than the usual number of people into the park. Top-hatted gentlemen and ladies with parasols strolled beneath the oaks and chestnuts. Nobles and newly-rich cantered down Rotten Row on horses that glistened like polished stone. Governesses in starched blouses whispered gossip to one another, breaking off now and then to reprimand their young charges, who clung to kite strings, dashed through games of tag, and were never as well-behaved as "proper" children ought to be. Robins and dunnocks hopped across the lawns, while flotillas of swans and geese, stately as ships of the line, patrolled the shallows of the Serpentine, heedless of the languid boaters drifting on the lake.

Chuggers drew up beside his partner. "If the doctor's going hunting, where's his horse?" the bear inquired.

"He don't mean fox hunting," Slatkin replied. "More like shooting."

"Oh, it's shooting we're about," said Chuggers, nodding. "Funny, I didn't figure the doctor to be such a sportsman." But then the bear grew puzzled again. "Does he mean to go shooting in Hyde Park?" he asked.

Slatkin shrugged.

"And what's he going to shoot with?" Chuggers went on. "He don't have a shotgun in this bag, that's for sure."

"Maybe he marches 'em to death," said Slatkin, breathing hard.

"And what game is it we're to be going after?" Chuggers continued. "Squirrels? Toads? We ain't after catching toads, are we? I don't like toads. A toad once bit me on the toe."

"Toads don't bite," said Slatkin. "They ain't got no teeth."

"You ain't got but a couple of teeth yourself," the bear countered. "But that don't stop you from gnawing away."

"But I ain't no toad, you feeble-brained bear!"

"So then maybe this toad pinched me," Chuggers speculated. "Anyways, it hurt. So I has good reasons not to like toads."

"We ain't after no toads," stated Slatkin, rolling his eyes.

"So what game is we after?"

"How should I know?" snapped the ferret, who felt certain that he did know and was not the happier for it. "Think the doctor tells me everything? Why don't you just walk along and save your breath for something that needs saying?"

Chuggers stuck out his lower lip. "I bet Sure Luck Holmes don't talk so sharp to his friend . . . and partner," he grumbled.

"Sherlock Holmes don't know how lucky he is," Slatkin muttered.

The hunting party traversed Hyde Park, passing through Speaker's Corner—where a bearded gentleman was orating on the subject of giving the vote to all English men, while denying it to all English women—then striking up Edgware Road. It was not until Dr. Van Detta turned onto Harrow Road that Slatkin was able to guess their destination.

Kensal Green Cemetery lay in state between the Grand Union Canal and Harrow Road. London's first public cemetery, it had been created by an act of Parliament in 1832 as an alternative to London's ancient churchyards, which had become so stuffed with corpses that it was no longer possible to ignore the stench or the threat of epidemic.

The doctor and the ferret passed right through the main gate, but Chuggers pulled up short.

"Pssst! Slatkin!" he whispered urgently.

The ferret turned about.

"What we doing in this cemet'ry?"

"Hunting for something, I suppose," Slatkin replied.

"What we hunting for in here?" asked Chuggers, looking perplexed.

"Vampires, of course," Slatkin answered, with a mischievous grin. *Ha!* he thought. *Just let that bit o' news sink to the bottom of that bear's muddy brain. Then watch him bolt!* He waited for Chuggers to react.

"Oh," said Chuggers. "All right, then."

Now it was Slatkin who was perplexed. "'All right then'?" he repeated. "Ain't you bothered about it?"

"Why should I be bothered?" asked Chuggers. "As I don't believe in vampires, I don't expect that we shall meet up with any."

Slatkin snatched his hat off his head. "And what if I was to tell you," he said, waving his bowler at the bear, "that this here doctor, who is an expert in these matters, believes with absolute certainty that there really are such things as vampires—including that very same hound which we is trying to find and which you had a hold of just last night? What would you say then?"

Chuggers thought this over. "I would say you needs to pay me more money," he replied.

Slatkin snorted indignantly and clapped his hat back on his head. Then he spun about and trotted after Dr. Van Detta, who had already plunged into the maze of monuments and disappeared.

"And I would say that even a expert can be wrong!" Chuggers shouted, before he, too, trotted to catch up.

When the partners next saw the doctor, he was speaking into an open grave. As they drew nearer, the head of the gravedigger popped into view.

"Nothing unusual?" Van Detta asked the man. "Especially around the new burials?"

The gravedigger's pick bit a chunk of clay from the bottom of the grave. "Nothin' that I seen," he said, without looking up.

"No signs of vampire activity?"

The gravedigger interrupted his next swing and turned his face to the doctor. Rivulets of sweat cut channels through the dirt on the man's cheeks. His gray mustache was flecked with clay. He tilted his head back, regarding the doctor with one eye closed. Finally, he said, "No, I ain't seen no vampires . . . nor unicorns, neither."

"Them's my sentiments," Chuggers whispered to Slatkin.

Van Detta refused to take offense. "Nevertheless, there may be vampires about," he said. "You would be wise to take precautions. If you suspect a corpse has a tendency toward vampirism, you should bury it facedown. That way, if it attempts to dig its way out, it will only dig deeper into the earth. Or you may bury it with a vast multitude of seeds. The vampire will feel compelled to count all the seeds before it can emerge."

"I'll do that, guvnuh," said the gravedigger, placing his tongue in his cheek and winking at Slatkin.

"In the meantime," the doctor went on, "I suppose you won't object if we inspect the grounds for signs of the undead?"

"Be my guest," said the gravedigger. "But mind, don't you go flushing out no werewolves. Them's my department." Chuckling, the gravedigger returned to his work.

Dr. Van Detta led Slatkin and Chuggers through the graveyard. While most of the graves were marked by plain stone slabs, some of the deceased were commemorated by more elaborate monuments: miniature cathedrals and pyramids; marble tableaux of men and women, horses and dogs; even a large beehive. Obviously, several thousand pounds was considered a small price to pay to be noticed after death.

"Look here, Chuggers," said Slatkin, pointing to a simple stone cross. "This is the grave of Mr. Wilkie Collins."

"Who's he?" asked the bear.

"That writer chap. If memory serves, I burgled his house once."

"You always was more educated than me," said Chuggers admiringly. "If I had stuck to my schooling, I might have stolen from some writers myself."

The day wore on, the sun grew warmer, and Slatkin and Chuggers began to feel that they were being dragged in the doctor's wake like men being keelhauled. Van Detta kicked at mounds of earth and tried the doors of crypts but showed no particular interest in any tomb for very long. They stopped for a time to observe a burial service—until the black-clad mourners began to stare and cough with increasing irritation and the trio had to move on.

Suddenly, the doctor halted in front of a tomb. It was fashioned after a Greek temple, with Doric columns on all sides and a pediment featuring a statue of an angel lying facedown. Van Detta stared at the tomb, his forefinger stroking the curve of his nose.

"Did you find something, doctor?" asked the ferret, in a hushed tone.

"Note the angel," said Van Detta. "What would you make of that, Slatkin?"

The ferret cocked his head to one side. "Just an angel lying down," he concluded. "Maybe he's asleep."

"Or maybe he has fallen," said the doctor, his voice filled with meaning. "Perhaps he is a fallen angel, ergo Lucifer, the Prince of Darkness, patron of all vampires."

Slatkin scrutinized the statue. "No, I still think he's sleeping," the ferret decided.

But Van Detta would not be put off. "Note the name on the tomb," he continued. "'Lamie.' Is not *lamia* the ancient Greek word for a vampire?"

"Greek were never my area of expertise, sir," said Slatkin apologetically. "I have heard some sailors in Limehouse speaking Greek, though. Unless maybe it were Russian. . . ."

"This is no mere coincidence," the doctor stated, his eyes glinting with intense interest. "These are signs. Come, let us try the entrance to the crypt."

Van Detta hurried around to the rear of the tomb, with Slatkin and Chuggers trailing behind. There they found a rusting iron door leading to a crypt beneath the monument. The lock on the door had been broken.

"You see!" cried the doctor. "The tomb is open. Perhaps we may find our friends at home. Chuggers, bring me the bag!"

Chuggers passed the canvas bag to Van Detta, who placed it on a nearby slab and began extracting the contents. "Hang these about your neck," he ordered, handing each of his henchmen a wreath of garlic. He looped a similar wreath around his own neck.

"What we need these for?" asked Chuggers, wrinkling his nose.

"They will protect you from the vampire," said the doctor.

"They'll make me stink," the bear complained.

"Which would be an improvement," Slatkin remarked, with a nervous titter.

Next, Van Detta produced two large candles—one for the ferret, one for the bear—which he lit with a match. Last, he armed himself with three sharp wooden stakes, a wooden mallet, and a silver cross. "We are ready," he announced. The faces of his companions indicated that they were, perhaps, less ready than he.

"Show no fear, and do exactly as I command," the doctor warned them. "Chuggers, the door."

With one muscular arm, the bear drew back the iron door, which groaned as it came free. Stone steps led down into darkness.

"Slatkin, you will precede me, to light the way," Van Detta said.

Swallowing hard, the ferret placed one foot on the top step. "Ain't never burgled a tomb," he muttered, as he started his descent.

The air in the crypt was as thick as wool and smelled strongly of mold and decay. Cobwebs waved at Slatkin's face, making him shudder. He held his candle high. The feeble flame fell on the vaults of the dead, their names cast in bronze or etched in stone. Some tombs bore Biblical phrases—I SHALL NOT WANT or I AM THE RESURRECTION AND THE LIGHT—others were decorated with chiseled vines and rosettes.

Slatkin heard the rapid, excited breathing of the doctor immediately behind him, a tenor counterpoint to the rumbling wheeze of the bear. For his own part, the ferret could barely breathe at all.

Suddenly, there was a rustling in the darkness.

"What you want?"

A child's voice, beseeching and challenging at the same time. Instantly, Slatkin swung his candle toward the sound.

The boy was probably no more than ten or eleven, though too much of too little had added years to his face. His clothes were shabby and ill-fitting; the shirtsleeves threatened to engulf his hands, while the shirttail brushed against his knees. Bare toes protruded through cracks in his boots. He stood his ground, one fist balled at his side, his right hand clutching a length of iron pipe. Behind him, on a pallet made of leaves, newspaper, and old sacks, two smaller children peeked out from under a faded shawl. They appeared to be a boy and a girl; the most that could be said for certain was that they were frightened and underfed.

Dr. Van Detta rushed forward, brandishing his silver cross. "Stay back, children of darkness!" His voice rang in the narrow confines of the crypt.

The older boy took a step backward, raising his club to the ready. Despite the set of his jaw, the pipe trembled in his hand. "What do you want?" he repeated. "We ain't done nothing. We ain't causing no harm."

"These is vampires?" asked Chuggers doubtfully.

"Do not be fooled," the doctor warned. "These monsters can assume many shapes. Children can be infected like any other."

"Vampires?" said the boy. "You take us for vampires? Are you daft?"

"If you are a vampire, I will soon know," Van Detta countered. "Boy, hold out your arm."

"What for?"

"Hold out your arm!" The doctor's stern command made the younger children whimper.

Reluctantly, the boy raised his left arm. Van Detta seized the boy by the wrist and pushed back his sleeve. With a quick movement, he pressed the cross against the boy's chalky skin.

"Bring the light closer," the doctor ordered. Slatkin came forward. Van Detta removed the cross. He bent to study the boy's skin in the candlelight. He let the arm fall.

"The cross left no mark," the doctor said, with obvious disappointment. "This child is not a vampire."

"Of course I ain't," said the boy.

"I never thought so," Chuggers remarked.

"What you doing down here, boy?" Slatkin inquired.

"Waiting for a train," the boy replied.

"Don't be cheeky," Slatkin said. "I ain't looking to cause you no trouble. I just wants to know."

The boy looked at the smaller children, who edged nearer,

taking refuge behind his legs. "We live here is all," the boy explained quietly. "We got to live someplace, don't we?"

"Where are your parents?" Van Detta asked.

"Our dad were a soldier," the boy related. "He went to Africa four years ago. Mum said he weren't coming back. Then Mum, she died of coughing six months ago. She's buried in this cemetery, a little ways from here. There ain't no stone. Since Mum died, the twins and me been on our own."

"Cholera took my mum," Chuggers offered.

"You have no other relatives?" the doctor asked.

"None as want three more mouths to feed," the boy answered.

"Yes, I am familiar with that story," said Van Detta, nodding. "Still, you ought to be in school. There are laws in England, are there not?"

"I were in school, mostly, till Mum took sick," the boy said. "How can I go now? Who would look after these?" He tilted his head toward the twins.

"This don't seem a great place to live," said Slatkin, looking around. "Of course, I seen worse."

"It ain't such a bad place," the boy replied, "if you ain't scared o' ghosts. It's better than sleeping out of doors. And it ain't so far from Mum. We likes that, especially the twins. You ain't going to make us leave, are you?"

Slatkin and Chuggers looked to Van Detta.

"Whether you live here or not is entirely your affair," the doctor stated. "Chuggers, light the way out." He turned to go.

"Excuse me, sir," said the boy.

Van Detta halted. "What is it?"

"Could you spare a few coppers, sir? Anything at all?"

Five faces turned expectantly to the doctor.

Van Detta's gaze traveled from the wretched boy to the equally wretched siblings. For an instant, pity flickered in the doctor's eyes. The emotion passed, however, and the doctor's reply was matter-of-fact. "Life is hard, boy. If you want to raise your station, you must do as I did—you must fight your way up. I wish you luck." Snatching the candle from Chuggers, he stalked away.

Slatkin turned to the children. Their hopeful expressions had vanished; once again they wore the dull gray mask of poverty. It was a face Slatkin had seen in tenements and alleys all over London, every day of his life.

The ferret dug into his pocket. Extracting three pennies, he handed them to the boy.

"Thank you, sir," said the boy. "You is most kind."

"No bother," said Slatkin. "You look after them little ones now."

"I will, sir. I'll do the best by them that I can."

Slatkin and Chuggers turned their backs on the orphans and headed out of the crypt. As Slatkin mounted the stairs ahead of him, Chuggers said, "It were good of you to give 'em those coins."

"It were nothing," Slatkin muttered, "and next-to-nothing is what it will do for them."

"Oh, it were something, all right," Chuggers affirmed. "And something is always better than nothing . . . unless we is speaking of boils or bedbugs or such like, in which case, some is always worse than none."

"Which could be said of your conversation," Slatkin complained.

"Speaking of nothing," Chuggers went on, "didn't you tell me previous that you was all out of money? Yet you give that boy three coppers."

Slatkin stopped climbing and turned around, his face level with the bear's. "Don't you trust me, Chuggers?" he demanded. "'Cause if you don't, maybe we ought to dissolve this partnership right here and now."

Chuggers was taken aback. "Why, of course I trusts you, Slatkin," he replied, with sincerity. "Long as I've known you, you been as honest a crook as a bloke could ever meet.

Whatever games you plays with the rest of the world, I know you always plays straight with me."

"You mean that?" asked Slatkin.

"I truly do," Chuggers answered.

"All right, then," said Slatkin. "Do you still have the tuppence I give you this morning?"

The bear felt in his pocket. "I do," he said.

"Give it to me."

"What for?" Chuggers asked.

"Because, from now on, I am the partner in charge of getting, spending, and all matters otherwise monetary."

Chuggers hesitated.

"You said you trusted me," Slatkin reminded him.

"And I meant it," the bear affirmed, placing the coin in Slatkin's paw. "I only held back to see if you was really sincere in wanting it."

"Right," said the ferret, with a sniff.

"So, tell me, Slatkin—does you trust me?"

The ferret rubbed his cheek. He coughed twice and spat. He adjusted his hat.

"Well?" Chuggers pressed.

"To the best of my knowledge, I do," Slatkin replied.

"Do you mean it?"

"I said it, didn't I?"

"So, if you is in charge of the money," asked Chuggers, "then what am I in charge of?"

Slatkin placed a paw on Chuggers's shoulder and looked him in the eye. "You is in charge of doing everything what I says to do."

The bear stared at the ferret. Then he nodded his head slowly. "I believes I can handle that," he said.

"Good!" Slatkin answered brightly. He thumped the bear on the chest. "I think this partnership is going to work out after all."

At that point, a red-faced Dr. Van Detta appeared at the top of the stairs. "The dead move faster than you two!" he barked. "Come on! This is not the only cemetery in London!"

"Coming, sir," Slatkin replied. "We was just making extra certain there weren't no vampires down here."

"You were just wasting my time! Hurry up!" The doctor stomped off.

"I must say, that doctor don't seem like the pleasantest person," Chuggers remarked.

"Oh, that's only a first impression," Slatkin replied. "Once you get to know him, you'll find that he's just plain mean."

VII

Tea for Tilney

If Fate had made Barksdale a vampire, it had also made him a gentleman. A distant relative on his mother's side—a gentleman hound his mother could barely remember and Barksdale himself had never met—had generously, miraculously bequeathed his estate in Ireland to young Barksdale. The income from the estate had provided a comfortable living for Barksdale and his mother and allowed the hound to be educated as a gentleman. Subsequently, it allowed him to pursue the work of a gentleman—a gentleman's work normally consisting of speaking well, dressing well, dining well, riding well, and marrying well. In that regard, Mr. Barksdale spoke well, dressed as well as he liked, dined simply, rode when he had to, and had never tried marriage. To his credit, he also believed that a gentleman—or anyone— ought to do something that mattered.

As a gentleman, Barksdale was entitled to a staff of domestic servants. The hound, however, had decided early on that a large staff might not be best for a gentleman with his peculiar "condition." Therefore, at Harker Place, there was no butler, no footman, no valet, no housekeeper, no parlor maid, no upstairs maid, no scullery maid, and no cook. There was only Tilney Potts, the indispensable Potts, performing the duties of an entire staff with diligence, with competence, and lately, with one arm in a sling.

It was Wednesday, and Tilney had the afternoon off. He strolled down Oxford Street, left arm in the sleeve of his coat, right arm slung close to his body. It had been two weeks since his injury, and the pain was hardly noticeable, but Dr. Mullbender had advised him to continue wearing the sling for another week. On this day, a persistent breeze set the empty coat sleeve flapping, forcing Tilney to grip it tightly with his right paw.

The little rat glimpsed himself in a shop window. *You are a sight,* he thought, chuckling softly. *A one-armed, bobtailed rat with a yellow and purple eye. What must people think? You are either some sort of ne'er-do-well or you have wandered away from the Chelsea army hospital.* He decided that he would imagine himself as a wounded war hero, and everyone else could think as they liked.

Now, this particular Wednesday was also the second Wednesday of the month, and on the second and fourth Wednesdays of every month, Tilney Potts traveled to the home of his sister Nan for afternoon tea. Like many of Tilney's relatives, Nan lived with her family in Cheapside, in the shadows of those two great bastions of authority, Newgate Prison and St. Paul's Cathedral. It was a poor neighborhood, where children played in trash-filled alleyways that never felt the sun (though it was not so bad as parts of Clerkenwell or Spitalfields—not to mention South London, where filth ran amok). Nan's husband, Fred, was a decent, hardworking rat, who tried to support his family on the slim proceeds of a small cheese shop. To bring in extra money, Nan and her two older daughters did sewing work. London had a booming garment business, and there was always a great deal to sew, if very little pay to reap.

Nan's normally warm welcome became a gasp of horror when she saw her brother's injuries.

"I'm fine, really," Tilney assured her, as Nan carefully removed his coat. "It looks much worse than it is."

"It looks bad enough," Nan fretted. She guided her brother to a chair slouching beside the kitchen table. "Oh, this old chair wobbles so. Maybe we should get you another."

From his regular visits, Tilney knew as well as his sister that the wobbling chair was actually the sturdiest piece of furniture in the room. It certainly appeared more robust than the sagging cupboard, the lurching table, and the other crippled chairs. In fact, the entire flat seemed in need of a crutch.

"This chair is perfectly fine, Nan," Tilney insisted, as he carefully took his seat. "Please, don't trouble yourself."

At the sound of Tilney's voice, Nan's children came spilling through the curtain that separated the family's single bedroom from the kitchen-parlor.

"Uncle Tilney!" they cried. Heedless of the rat's injuries, they nearly knocked him off his chair in their eagerness to give him a hug.

"Children! Children!" Nan fussed. "Mind, your uncle's been hurt."

Nan and Fred had five children: three girls and two boys. The eldest girl was busy helping Fred in the front room, which served as the cheese shop. The other four now stopped to gape at their uncle.

"Uncle Tilney, what happened?" asked Liza, five, touching the rat's injured arm gently, as if it were a bird's wing.

Tilney blushed. "It was nothing. Nothing at all."

"It were most obviously something," said Nan, with concern. "Nothing does not leave such marks on a person."

"A minor scrape," Tilney replied. He would have left it at that, but the expectant faces of his audience convinced him to say more. "Another fellow and I went to the defense of a young woman," he explained. "Her assailants objected to our interference, and things got a bit rough. Fortunately, we prevailed. That was the entire matter. But I'm much better already. See?" Tilney slipped his right arm from the sling and waved it at the children.

"Tilney Potts, you put that arm back!" Nan ordered him. "You will make things worse."

"You is a hero, Uncle Tilney," said Daniel, six.

Tilney blushed again. "There was nothing heroic about it," he replied. "My friend did all the work. Had it not been for him, I might be in worse shape than I am."

"You is too modest," said Nan.

"You are too kind," Tilney told her. "Now, shall we have some tea?"

"I'll put the water on," said Nan. She took up the teakettle and filled it from the pipe in the kitchen. "We have water from the pipe now all the time," she marveled. "They've fixed it for the whole neighborhood. I know some people say this town will never do a poor man right, but there it is—running water, day or night." She set the kettle to boil on the grate over the small fireplace that served as their stove.

Seeing Nan and the children in their cramped kitchen, Tilney Potts felt a familiar twinge of embarrassment—embarrassment that he should live so comfortably, while his sister and her family lived so hard. When he had first come to tea, he had been sure to bring some tarts, pots of jam, or lemon cake. He might even—with his master's blessing—provide bacon, eggs, or ham from Mr. Barksdale's pantry. Nan and Fred had been deeply grateful for the gifts, of course. But Tilney could tell from the way they lowered their eyes that his generosity made them feel ashamed of their own poverty. He was afraid that, in time, this shame would turn to resentment. So he had stopped bringing gifts to Nan's, except for a sack of sweets for the children, which all could accept happily.

The water boiled; the tea was brewed. Fred and his daughter Molly came in from the shop to join them. Fred was a tall rat, who, in spite of his hardships, looked out on life with a pleasant expression. He had a short brown mustache and wispy eyebrows that hopped about whenever he became excited. Molly, sixteen, was tall like her father, with long, curling whiskers and auburn hair. She was pretty—not people-pretty or bird-pretty or even flower-pretty, but rat-pretty, which is a lucky thing, if you are a rat.

"How goes the cheese business, Fred?" asked Tilney.

"Good and bad, Tilney. Bad and good. Like all business, I suppose. I'm sure it will only get better. I have hopes for my stock of double Gloucestershire. It brought in thruppence just this morning."

As he gave his answer, Fred leaned on the kitchen table, causing it to list to the east, like a ship on a rolling sea. Nan, who was bustling around the kitchen, promptly checked the tilting table with her hip and shoved it back to perpendicular.

"Sounds like business is booming, Fred," Tilney teased. "Now, mind you don't nibble your stock down to nothing."

"No fear of that," Fred replied. "Cheese is such a worry to me that I'm afraid I can barely stomach it."

"Ain't your family a worry, too, Fred Hodge?" his wife remarked. "But you ain't sickened by us, I hope."

Fred patted Nan's thick forearm. "Worry I might, but I shall never tire o' my own," he said.

Nan and her daughters laid cracked cups and chipped plates on the shuddering table. Nan sliced some bread, then spread each slice with drippings. Finally, she poured the tea.

Tilney sipped and pronounced the tea "excellent."

Nan beamed with pleasure. "It's real Indian," she said proudly. "Mrs. Jenkins give it me for the two dresses I sewed for her. You have to be so careful about tea, you know. There's so many fakers out there, filling teabags with sand and dirt and who knows what."

"World's full of charlatans," Fred declared. "Just the other day, a bloke come into my shop and tried to buy some cheese with what he said was a 'new shilling coin.' Said it was only just issued by Her Majesty's mint; that's why I'd never seen its like before."

"And was it a new shilling?" asked Tilney.

"It coulda been," Fred stated, looking sideways at his wife. "But it were actually more of a coat button."

"I hope you showed him the door," said Tilney.

"Oh, he showed him the door, all right," Nan reported, in a scolding tone. "Showed him right out the door with a shilling's worth of cheese!"

Fred hung his head. "Well, that bloke had an honest face," he mumbled.

"Many a person's got an honest face who ain't got an honest heart!" Nan declared loudly. "Guy Fawkes like to had an honest face, right before he tried to blow up Parliament!"

"Mummy, did you know Guy Fawkes?" asked Daniel.

The question caught Nan off guard. She immediately forgot about haranguing her husband and cast a bemused look at Daniel. "Does your mother look three hundred years old?" she asked her son, while Tilney, Fred, and the older children fought to keep from giggling.

"No, Mummy," Daniel replied. "You don't look half that."

"Thank you, dear," she said, patting Daniel on the head. "I wasn't certain that I looked even that good."

Tilney took this opportunity to change the subject. "Any family news?" he asked.

"Nothing yet from Will and Tom," Nan said, referring to Tilney's older brothers. "I should think they would have arrived in Cape Town by now."

"They'll send word soon, I'm certain," Tilney assured her.

"Southern Africa's the coming thing," Fred opined. "Gold and diamonds sticking up out the ground. A man could make a fortune there."

"Don't you be getting any ideas, Fred," said his wife. "I'd as soon move to the moon. And you ain't going alone."

"I weren't getting no ideas, Nan," Fred countered. "You know I never get ideas."

"Anything else?" Tilney interjected.

Nan put her paw to her nose, thinking. "Well, Uncle Edgar has it in mind to do something special for the Queen's Diamond Jubilee. He wants to grow a turnip that looks like Her Majesty. Can you imagine that? I'm not sure Her Majesty would be flattered."

"Oh, she's a good old girl," Fred remarked. "I'm certain she wouldn't take it amiss. You know, Tilney, Uncle Edgar's plan set me to thinking: do you suppose a round of cheese could be carved in the shape of Her Majesty?" His eyebrows began to twitch.

"I'm certain that cheese is every bit as good for sculpting as marble," said Tilney, while his sister shook her head. "The great advantage of cheese is, if Her Majesty should not have room for the cheese portrait at Buckingham Palace or Balmoral, she can always eat it."

Fred gave this point serious consideration. "Of course," he commented, "I might not be able to spare the inventory."

"I should think not," Nan responded firmly. "Nor the time, Fred."

Fred wiped the crumbs from his mustache. "Speaking of which, I had best attend to business." He rose from the table, which tipped forward, so that Tilney had to catch his plate before it landed in his lap. "Dame Fortune may come through the door at any moment."

"Any paying customer would do," said Nan.

Fred nodded to Tilney and went back to work.

"Molly, you'd better go, too," Nan told her daughter. "Your father may need your help. You know he has a way of misplacing money."

Molly's shoulders slumped. "But, Mother, it's so boring," she groaned. "Can't I stay awhile and listen to Uncle Tilney? He always has such interesting things to tell." She smiled at her uncle, hoping to enlist his support.

"Your father needs looking after, girl," Nan reminded her. "And I can't be two places at once."

"But it's just cheese and more cheese in the shop," Molly complained.

"I know it ain't exciting work for a young girl," said her mother. "But might not a young, handsome rat come in for a slice of cheese? And what good will it do you, if you're hidden in the kitchen talking to your uncle?"

"Well, he ain't come in yet," Molly argued. "And if I work in the shop a million years, he probably won't never come then, either!"

Her mother gave her a severe look. Molly frowned but stood up from the table and went to join her father.

"That girl is too headstrong for her own good," Nan declared.

"She must take after her mother," said Tilney, with a sly smile.

Nan pretended to be angry. "You are nothing but a scamp, brother. You toy with all of us, and Fred most of all. You know he takes everything you say to heart."

"I'm sorry, Nan," Tilney apologized, still smiling. "I only tease Fred because I like him. He is married to my favorite sister, after all." At this, Nan smiled, too. "Besides, I know you won't let him go astray."

"I'm not worried about Fred," said Nan. "It's you what needs watching over."

By now the children had slurped the last drops of their tea, wiped the last breadcrumbs from their plates, and become bored with this line of conversation.

"Uncle Tilney," said Peter, who was eight, "last time you started telling us about your current master. Will you tell us more?"

"Yes! Tell us more!" echoed Liza. "Is he really an Indian raja?"

"Is that what I said last time?" Tilney asked.

"It is," Peter affirmed.

"Yes, indeed," Tilney replied. "He is the raja of Ramapoor, one of the richest and most mysterious regions of India."

"Ramapoor?" Peter questioned. "I seen a map of India in the

newspaper just yesterday. I don't recall seeing no Ramapoor on the map."

"It's not on the map," Tilney said, with authority. He lowered his voice. "That's what makes it so mysterious."

"Why is the raja here in England?" asked Daniel. "If I were a raja, I'd stay in India and hunt tigers all the time."

"As would my master, if he had the choice," Tilney stated. "But, you see, my master's evil stepbrother has stolen the throne of Ramapoor, forcing my master to flee. Naturally, my master came to England, to seek the help of Her Majesty."

"Why did he hire you, Uncle?" asked Franny, twelve, as she cleared the table. "Didn't he bring his own servants?"

"He was barely able to escape with his life," Tilney explained. "He took only his turban and a chest of rubies. And his pet cobra."

"His pet cobra!" gasped Daniel. "Who would keep a cobra for a pet? They're terrible poisonous."

"Oh, this cobra is perfectly tame," Tilney assured his nephew. "He coils atop my master's head and shoos the flies away with a peacock feather. And he spoons the sugar into my master's tea. And, of course, he can play card games; if you win, however, he hisses quite rudely."

"Uncle Tilney," said Peter, with a skeptical look, "are you making this up?"

"Oh, no, Peter," Tilney replied, with great seriousness. "It's absolutely true. I would never try to fool a lad as bright as you."

"What's his name?" asked Liza.

"Who?"

"The snake."

"The snake?" said Tilney. He hesitated. "His full name is Tooma-loopa-gooma-noopa. But everyone calls him Bertie because he looks so much like the Prince of Wales."

"How can a snake look like the Prince of Wales?" asked Daniel.

"It is hard to believe," Tilney acknowledged. "But if you ever saw this snake in a morning coat, you would be struck by the resemblance."

"Will Her Majesty help your master get his kingdom back?" asked Franny.

"Her Majesty is a most sympathetic monarch," said Tilney. "As soon as she heard my master's sorry tale, she dispatched an order to Horse Guards. At this very moment, her generals are preparing their battle plans and the Grenadier Guards are sharpening their bayonets. It would not surprise me if the Duke of Wellington himself were to command the expedition."

The children were awed by this information.

"But the Duke of Wellington is long since dead," Peter objected.

"For a matter of this importance, he would gladly revive," Tilney said quickly. He drew a small sack from his pocket. "Now, does anyone have a taste for sugarplums?"

The children responded eagerly. "Take yourselves outside," their mother insisted, "so your uncle and I may have a talk without your lip-smacking."

The children thanked Tilney and rushed out to the alley with their treats.

Nan sat down at the table. She had broad shoulders and heavy arms, like their father. Her hair, which Tilney had combed as a child, was almost completely gray now. She pulled it into a bun at the back of her head, but some of the strands refused to be collected and coiled like springs beside her cheeks.

"The children believes you, you know," Nan said to her brother.

"A little fairy tale will do them no harm," Tilney replied.

"The truth is mysterious enough," said Nan. "You tell us nothing about the man you work for."

"I have told you his name," Tilney countered.

"Aye, Barksdale," Nan confirmed. "And that is all you has

told. And that little bit you have made me swear not to repeat to anyone—not even Fred."

"Not even Fred," Tilney reminded her.

"It's this secrecy what gives everyone wrong ideas," Nan complained. "You know Father strongly disapproves of your position. He believes your master is not a proper gentleman. He thinks he must be a criminal, else why all this keeping in the dark?"

"Father wanted me to work the colliers alongside himself and my brothers," Tilney replied. "He was bound to disapprove of anything else I might do."

"You could have been a coal-whipper, you know," said Nan. "I'll grant it's hard work . . . "

Tilney shook his head. "Not after the accident, Nan. I had nightmares for months. The net breaking, Father shouting, the coal pouring down. In the dreams it buried all of me, not just my tail. I knew I could never go near those ships again."

Nan sighed. "It were unfortunate. Now Father says you don't even speak like us no more. He says we're not to speak of you, as you've turned your back on us."

"Not on you, Nan." Leaning forward, Tilney covered her paw with his.

"It's hard," said Nan, her eyes glistening. "It's hard to hear Father speak so of you. It's hard to know you think ill of Father. How am I to do right by both of you?"

"I'm sorry, Nan," Tilney murmured. "I know it is hard. I know I have put you in the middle. But I know you will always be a good sister and a good daughter." He gave her an impish look. "Or I shall dip your tail in paint as I did when I was five."

Nan brightened at the recollection. "Are you certain this Mr. Barksdale is a proper gentleman?" she inquired.

"He is the best and kindest gentleman I have ever met," Tilney stated. "When I was injured, he nursed me himself. I could give you so many examples . . ." The rat paused, as if uncertain whether to go on.

"Yes?" said Nan.

Tilney hesitated a moment longer, then plunged ahead. "Do you remember when Liza had the croup?" he asked.

"Two winters ago," Nan recalled.

"It was Mr. Barksdale who insisted on sending the doctor, Mr. Barksdale who paid the fee."

Nan was astounded. "I never knew," she said, after a moment. "I couldn't imagine who, but then I thought perhaps you . . . " She looked solemnly at her brother. "We owe your Mr. Barksdale a great debt, then. Liza would have died without that doctor."

"That's not all," Tilney went on. "The Home for Incurables in Clapham Road . . . The St. Giles Boys Refuge . . . they both receive regular donations from Mr. Barksdale. And he does many other good works throughout London."

"I had no idea," said Nan. "But why must this all be kept secret?"

"Because Mr. Barksdale wishes it to be," Tilney replied. "I trust you will respect his wishes. I have told too much already, I'm afraid. But I wanted to put you, at least, in the right."

"It is Father who needs convincing," Nan argued.

"Father must trust in me," Tilney told her, "as I trust in Mr. Barksdale."

Brother and sister drank a second cup of tea. Then it was time for Tilney to go.

"You'll come again?" Nan asked, as she helped Tilney into his coat.

Tilney hugged his sister with his free arm. "Again and again, Nan," he assured her. "Tell Fred I wish him luck with his sculpting."

"Off with you, troublemaker!" his sister ordered, but she was laughing as she pushed him out the door.

VIII

Found Again

Slatkin and Chuggers reclined on a stack of packing crates in an alley on the north side of New Oxford Street.

"Another carrot?" asked Slatkin, offering the bunch to his companion. He and Chuggers had helped a costerman fix a wheel on the man's donkey cart; the carrots were their payment.

"Might as well," said Chuggers. "You has already had four."

"Three!" Slatkin countered. "As many as you has had."

"Seemed like four to me," said the bear.

"Well, it were three," Slatkin insisted. "Which you would know, if you could count."

"I can count as good as some," Chuggers declared. "Maybe I ain't good at counting carrots is all."

"How'd I get you for a partner?" asked the ferret grumpily.

"Same as I got you for a friend," the bear replied. "Have another carrot."

Slatkin accepted another carrot, brushed the dirt away, and bit off the end with a sharp crack. He watched the traffic passing on the street. His stomach rumbled. "When was the last time you had a real feast?" he asked.

Chuggers chewed thoughtfully. "Mum used to make plum pudding at Christmas," he said.

"Is that the last you can remember?"

"I once did a job in Belgravia," the bear recalled, "and I decided to raid the pantry while I was there. Oh, that were like heaven. I never seen so much food in one house. I ate a whole ham and a case of peach preserves. I ate so much, I got sleepy. The butler found me snoozing on the floor next morning. I were just able to scamper away before the peelers arrived."

"I never feel like eating when I'm on the job," Slatkin observed. "Must be my nerves. The last good meal I had was when they feasted us in honor of the Queen's Golden Jubilee. Ham and beef, puddings and pies, and plenty to wash it down. That were good eating."

The ferret pulled off his boots and massaged his toes. "How many miles has we walked these weeks past?" he asked, grimacing. "Chelsea, Westminster, Mayfair, Soho—we been everywhere and back again, day and night. We been to more cemet'ries than an undertaker's horse. If I'd knowed we was going to do all this marching, I'd've joined the army and got fed for it."

"And we still ain't had one more whiff of that hound," Chuggers added.

"Nor any other vampire," said Slatkin. "Which means the doctor ain't had no one but us to abuse. I didn't know I was hired to be his whipping boy."

"I bet Mr. Sure Luck Holmes would've found that hound by now," Chuggers reflected, with a sigh.

"Sherlock Holmes," Slatkin corrected him.

"Just as I said," the bear replied.

"No—Oh, never mind. Mr. Holmes would never have taken this case, I reckon."

They went back to nibbling their carrots. Slatkin gazed idly at the traffic: cabs and buses; coaches and carts; wagons hauling beer, bricks, water, trash, wood, coal, furniture, chickens, or anything else you could think of. The parade of vehicles was unbroken. It was like watching one of those "panorama" shows, only the painted pictures rolled on without end.

And then, suddenly, there was a moment's break in the traffic. Like a curtain parting, the wagons rolled away, and Slatkin could see clear across to the south side of New Oxford Street, where a little rat was walking along the pavement. At that moment, a gust of wind pushed the rat's coat from his shoulder, revealing an arm in a sling and a truncated tail.

The ferret leaped up. "Chuggers!" he cried. "It's him!" Frantically, Slatkin tried to wrestle his boots onto his feet. But he lost his balance, toppled off the pile of crates, and landed facedown in the alley.

"Who is it?" demanded Chuggers, his good eye wide as a gold sovereign. "The doctor? I ain't looking at no more graves. I seen enough dead people to last a lifetime."

"No, no!" barked Slatkin, scrambling to his feet. "The rat! The hound's rat! Come on!" Still trying to don his boots, the ferret hopped out of the alley.

Chuggers rolled slowly off the stack. "This detective business is too much hurrying," he said wearily, "and not enough larking about. But I still ain't larking!" he shouted, as if Slatkin could hear. Munching the remaining carrots, Chuggers sauntered after his partner.

Any reasonable being who has had a moral upbringing is bound to suspect that he or she possesses at least a few of the cardinal virtues. Tilney Potts, who was both reasonable and well brought-up, was confident that he had an honest and trustworthy nature. If he required proof, he need only look to the trust placed in him by Mr. Barksdale. His master's complete faith in him was a source of great pride to the little rat.

Like any reasonable and moral being, Tilney also possessed a conscience. And that conscience had been nagging him ever since he had left Nan's flat.

I said too much, he accused himself. *I should not have told those details about Mr. Barksdale. What if his nature were to become public knowledge? That one word*—vampire—*that's all people would see and hear. It would be enough to drive him from the city, or worse.*

And yet, how could he go on deceiving Nan? How could he keep the whole truth from someone who loved and trusted him so completely? Nan would always be understanding, Tilney knew; but she could be hurt, too. Since they were children, Nan had been willing to open her heart to him; she could not entirely forgive Tilney for hiding things from her now.

The little rat sighed heavily. It is a hard thing for an honest nature to be burdened with lies.

And then there was his father. Ephraim Potts had three sons and five daughters. He loved them all, but Tilney had been his favorite. It was Tilney who had cleaned and filled his father's pipe; Tilney who had read the Bible or the sporting pages to him in the evening. On Sundays during Tilney's youth, the whole family used to walk by the Thames. Tilney's brothers would scrabble along the muddy banks, searching for little treasures heaved up by the river. Tilney would sit quietly beside his father, while Ephraim watched the kaleidoscope of passenger steamers, colliers, lighters, and barges on the river. Sometimes he would look at Tilney and smile, patting the little rat's knee. Tilney never felt closer to his father than he did at those times. It was as if those Sundays on the riverbank had been created just for the two of them.

One sunny Sunday, Tilney's father had rowed them both downriver to the great Victoria Dock, a man-made anchorage deep enough to hold the largest oceangoing steamships.

"Look there, Tilney," his father had said, pointing to the rows of ships waiting to be loaded and unloaded. "It's as if all the oceans and all the rivers of the world flow into the Thames.

This river is the lifeblood of the city. You'll always find work on the river, if you're willing to bend your back."

His father had always been willing to break his back on the river. But Ephraim Potts had not foreseen that the great dock he admired would eventually steal his livelihood. The steam colliers that once had anchored in the pool of London, where coal-whippers like Ephraim Potts emptied their holds, were gradually diverted to Victoria Dock, where the coal could be unloaded faster and more cheaply by men working hydraulic cranes. As less and less coal reached the city docks, the London coal-whippers were forced to scramble for work on the city wharves. Sometimes they found work; often they were turned away. Tilney learned to tell by his father's walk whether he had earned any money that day. And yet, Ephraim Potts would not abandon the river.

Tilney, on the other hand, had never wanted to work on the river. Not after the accident, in any case. After the accident, the thought of standing in the bow of a lighter, riding out to bump against the bulk of a collier—it made him ill. It wasn't that he was afraid of hard work. Tilney could do hard work. Certainly, it was the accident.

But perhaps it was something more, Tilney admitted to himself. *Perhaps I have always wanted to be different. Perhaps the accident was Fate's way of granting my wish.*

Whatever the reason, his father had not understood. Ephraim Potts loved the river. He loved Tilney. How could his son not love what he loved?

The wind gusted along New Oxford Street. It brushed Tilney's coat from his right shoulder. The little rat halted. Reaching around with his good arm, he pulled the coat back to his shoulder and shrugged it into place. He continued walking, and thinking.

A crash interrupted Tilney's meditation. Looking up, he saw that the rear axle of a lumber wagon had split in two, causing its load of planks to slide into the street. The carter jumped down from his seat. Sputtering with anger, he kicked at the scattered wood, while his pair of mules, freed of their heavy load, swung their heads happily.

As Tilney watched, traffic began to pile up around the accident and a crowd gathered. Several men shouted advice to the driver, though no one went so far as to lend a hand. "I knew this city were getting too crowded; they's building right in the middle of the street now!" joked one man. "Here comes a ironmonger's wagon," said another. "Maybe he'll spill some nails to go with your wood!" These remarks drew bursts of laughter from everyone except the carter. The growing crowd attracted the notice of a wandering German band, which began playing loudly, ever hopeful that someone in the audience would pay them to go away.

Suddenly, Tilney's gaze fixed on two figures in the crowd across New Oxford Street. The taller figure—the bear—was idly munching a carrot and grinning at the amusing drama in the street. But the ferret—the ferret was staring straight at Tilney with an expression of intense interest.

A bolt of recognition flashed through Tilney's brain. Turning, he began to walk away as fast as he was able. As he did, he saw the ferret grab the bear by the arm and follow after him.

Tilney's short legs were not built for speed. The ferret and the bear soon drew even with him, though they remained on the other side of the street.

What could they want? Tilney worried. *Money? Revenge?* He hoped it was merely money; revenge was certain to be more painful.

Block after block, the pair stayed with him. When Tilney stopped, pretending to look in a shop window, the ferret and the bear halted, too.

What can I do? thought Tilney. *I am not far from home. But how can I go home? If I do, they will follow. They will know where I live. Who knows what trouble that may bring? I wish Mr. Barksdale were here!*

By now New Oxford Street had become Oxford Street. Harker Place was not far ahead. The ferret and the bear still shadowed him. Tilney was at a loss. He must do something. He needed time to think.

Desperate, he turned abruptly into the nearest doorway.

The shop was cool and dark. Taking off his hat, Tilney sagged against the door, grateful for a moment's relief. He peeked around the doorjamb. The ferret and the bear had halted. They were watching the door, but so far they were making no attempt to cross the street. Tilney let out a sigh.

"May I help you, sir?" said a soft female voice.

Tilney straightened. The shopgirl, a dormouse, stepped out from behind a row of tailor's dummies. She eyed the rat timidly.

"No, uh . . . well, perhaps," stammered Tilney. "I'm . . . looking."

"For what, sir?"

"A back door," Tilney blurted. "Do you have a back door?"

"I'm afraid not, sir," said the dormouse.

Tilney's whiskers drooped with disappointment. "I do wish you had a back door," he muttered.

"I'm very sorry, sir," the dormouse said. "You are the first customer to ask for a back door. May I show you something else?"

Tilney glanced through the window. His pursuers were slouching against a shopfront across the street. What was he to do? He needed ideas. His cousin Elijah—there was a rat with ideas.

I remember when Buffalo Bill's Wild West Show opened in Earl's Court, Tilney thought to himself. *Elijah covered himself with brick dust and tried to pass himself off as one of the Indians in the show. That was a bold idea. They threw him out, of course, but it was a bold idea. Why can't I think of something like that?*

Whereupon, Tilney thought of something like that.

"I need some different clothes," he told the shopgirl.

"For your wife, sir?"

"No, no," said Tilney. "I'm not married, miss. I mean clothes for myself."

The dormouse stared in surprise. "But, sir," she replied slowly, "this shop only sells clothes for ladies."

Tilney's face froze. He looked around. All of the tailor's dummies were draped in ladies' wear. "Yes, you're right." He grinned stupidly. "I hadn't noticed that."

A look of concern passed over the dormouse's squirrel-like features. She retreated behind one of the displays. "I suppose you'll be going then, sir?" she asked.

Tilney checked the ferret and the bear. They were still on guard. He turned in little circles, pulling at his whiskers, thinking.

What to do, what to do? I can't outrun them, and I can't hide in here forever. I must slip by them somehow. But how?

He had another idea. It was a ridiculous idea—but it was better than no idea at all.

Tilney cleared his throat. "Young lady," he said. "I see I must take you into my confidence."

The dormouse peeked around the folds of a green satin dress.

"I am Inspector Potts of Scotland Yard," Tilney declared.

The shopgirl gaped in awe. "The Yard?" she said.

"The Yard. Now, do you see those two rough-looking characters skulking across the street?"

The dormouse looked through the glass. "That bear and that ferret, you mean, sir?"

"Precisely. Young lady, they are two of the most notorious blackguards you can imagine."

The dormouse gasped. "You mean they're French, sir?"

"Uh . . . exactly," said Tilney. "They are French agents, and they are on my tail. And I must tell you, miss, that it is vital for the continued safety and well-being of Her Majesty's government that I elude these men."

"Oh, sir, if only we had a back door!" the dormouse lamented.

"That is no matter," said the rat. "I have a plan. This is what we must do."

So it was that, twenty minutes later, a small woman carrying a wrapped parcel exited the dress shop. She wore a yellow cotton dress, the hem hastily shortened, yet left long enough to cover a pair of masculine boots. Her shoulders were wrapped in a green shawl, while a yellow scarf draped her head. Looking neither left nor right, the woman proceeded steadily up Oxford Street and was soon lost amid the crowd.

"What's he doing in there?" Chuggers grumbled, when the rat had not reappeared after some time. "Buying a dress for his old mum, ya think?"

Slatkin shrugged. "Who knows? Maybe he's sweet on the shopgirl."

"What if he's already gone out the back, while we been guarding the front?" Chuggers asked.

"I know these shops," said Slatkin. "Ain't no back doors. We'll just sit tight here. He'll have to come out eventually. When he does, we shall follow the rat back to his hole. Find the hole, find the hound." He snapped his fingers. "Case closed."

Chuggers rested his back against the bricks, his arms folded across his stomach. "That hound is as good as found," he declared. "We is some pair of detectives, ain't we?"

"We is some pair," Slatkin agreed.

Barksdale was coming out of the drawing room when he heard the front door slam. Peering over the stair railing, he was astonished to behold Tilney Potts, red-faced, sweating, and clad in a yellow dress.

"Well, Potts," said the hound, "what you do on your afternoon off is certainly your own business. But I must say, this is something of a surprise."

"I've had a bit of an adventure, sir," Tilney answered excitedly.

He made his way up the stairs, tripping on his skirt with every step.

"Come into the drawing room and tell me of it," Barksdale said. "Although I must remind you, it is highly improper for a woman to pay a call on a gentleman."

"I trust you will not ruin my reputation, sir," Tilney replied.

The rat quickly related all the details of the pursuit and his escape.

"Well done, Potts," said Barksdale, when Tilney had finished. "I commend you on your quick thinking. I believe you may have saved us from an even greater danger."

"How is that, sir?"

"There was another message for me in this morning's *Times*," the hound explained. "It said, 'Barksdale, did the bear frighten you away?' It was signed 'E.V.D.,' like the other."

"He mentioned the bear, sir?" said Tilney. "But how would Dr. Van Detta know about our altercation? . . . Unless he and those ruffians are acquainted."

"We must assume that is the case, Potts," Barksdale replied. "The ferret and the bear who followed you may well be in the doctor's employ."

"Then it is a very good thing that I lost them, sir."

"Indeed, Potts. But I am afraid they are getting too close. Perhaps I have not taken this matter seriously enough. It may be time for action."

Tilney nodded vaguely. The excitement of his escapade had passed out of him as he had recounted it to Mr. Barksdale. Now he felt flat and worn out.

"Did you visit your sister today?" asked the hound, changing the subject.

"Yes, sir," Tilney answered.

"She and her family are well, I hope?"

"Very well, thank you, sir."

"Any news?"

Tilney tried to recall what had been said; his visit with Nan now seemed to have happened several months ago.

"My nephew Francis would like to be a surgeon, sir. He is practicing by working in the market, where he cuts the heads off fish."

"Excellent training," said Barksdale. "And his patients never complain. Every physician should be so lucky. Any word from your brothers at the Cape?"

"Nothing yet, sir."

"I'm certain they are well. You'll hear soon, no doubt. Now, perhaps you would like to change before dinner."

"I would, sir," said Tilney. Rising from the chair, he once again caught his foot on the skirt, so that he nearly pitched forward. "I don't think I should like to wear skirts all the time, sir," Tilney remarked. "They get underfoot even more often than a rat's tail."

"You must remember that, Potts," said Barksdale, "next time you go shopping for a disguise."

"I will, sir. Would you like anything particular for dinner, sir?"

"Blood sausages," the hound replied promptly.

"Are you certain, sir?" asked the rat. "I could easily cook you up some fish."

Barksdale shook his head. "I have an appetite for the sausages, Potts."

"Very well, sir."

Tilney left the drawing room and climbed the stairs toward his quarters on the second floor. "Blood sausages," he whispered, his forehead crinkling with concern. "That's the vampire in him, demanding to be fed." Tilney didn't like it. His father wouldn't like it either, he supposed. Tilney had a sudden vision of Ephraim Potts, his mouth a tight line above his gray whiskers, his eyes as hard as coal. "So this is what you do," his father would say. "The bidding of a monster."

Tilney bit his lip. It was all too much of a muddle for one little rat.

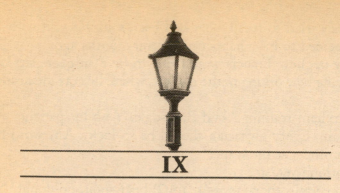

IX

Hunter and Hound

The butler helped Dr. Van Detta into his coat.

"I'll be dining out after the opera," said the doctor.

"Very good, sir," the butler replied. He handed the doctor his silk hat, gloves, and walking stick.

"Is the cab waiting?"

"As ordered, sir." The butler opened the door. "Have a pleasant evening, sir." The doctor said nothing and went out.

A two-wheeled hansom cab drawn by a piebald horse stood at the curb in front of the house. The horse was nibbling an apple offered by the cabman, a long-legged fellow in a black coat with the collar turned up. The driver's bowler hat was pulled low over his eyes and ears, while the rest of his face was obscured by whiskers black and bristling, like a chimney sweep's broom.

The cabman came to attention as Dr. Van Detta marched down the steps.

"Royal Opera House," said the doctor, barely glancing at the driver. Van Detta climbed into the open front of the cab and settled back on the seat. The driver climbed into the high seat at the rear of the cab. He flicked the reins, and the horse pulled into the street.

As usual, the streets were full of traffic. The cab started and stopped, crawled forward and, sometimes, backward. The doctor tapped his fingers impatiently on the pommel of his walking stick. The stick was made of polished ash wood, topped by a silver ball inscribed with the coat of arms of Otto, king of Bavaria. His Majesty had presented the walking stick to the doctor as a reward for tracking down the vampire of Nuremberg. The opposite end of the stick was encased in a brass cap. Beneath the cap, the wooden tip had been shaved to a sharp point—a point capable of piercing a vampire's heart, if necessary.

Van Detta knocked his stick against the roof of the cab. The driver opened the hatch. "Driver, is there no faster way?" the doctor called.

"I goes the fastest way I knows," the driver answered.

"He goes the way he can best cheat me on the fare," the doctor grumbled.

Van Detta closed his eyes and let the bouncing of the cab rock him into a brooding state of mind.

For nearly two months now I have marched back and forth across London, with nothing to show for it, he complained to himself. *Barksdale is here. I am certain of that. I feel the hound's presence in the city. I can almost smell him. But I cannot find him—nor any other vampire. This city has more than six million souls. Can I not find at least one that is undead?*

Things cannot continue in this way, he decided. *My sponsors are growing impatient. I receive a cable from Paris every day now, it seems. "How is the hunt?" they ask. "What is the progress? When may we expect results?"* The doctor snorted derisively. *What do they know about hunting vampires? They know nothing! All they desire are results, numbers, "This many hunted, this many destroyed." Something they can put in a ledger. To them, vampire hunting is nothing more than a public service, like rubbish collecting. They know nothing of the hardships. They are wealthy men. All they want is to get their money's worth.*

If he could not produce, they would take up one of his competitors—DeSantis, perhaps, or even Gunderson. Gunderson was an amateur, to be sure, but even an amateur might get lucky. Hadn't Gunderson stumbled upon that vampire banker in Vienna?

"Gunderson!" Van Detta muttered with disgust. *It's a hard business. Always on the move. Vicious competition. Late hours. No time for family or friends. Not to mention the constant risk of infection. The public has no idea what it is like.*

The doctor drew a deep breath and let it out slowly. *Relax*, he told himself. *Relax, and refresh your mind.* He needed a diversion. That's why he had decided to attend the opera. Perhaps the music would soothe him. What were they presenting tonight? Wagner? Wagner could be sublime. Let Wagner carry him beyond his cares. On the other hand, should the opera prove uninteresting—here he patted his coat pocket—he had brought along a copy of Shenk's *The Vampire Chickens of Ulm*.

Always there are new techniques to learn, he reminded himself. *I must keep up.*

The cab, which had been rolling slowly along the Mall, suddenly veered down Northumberland Avenue toward the river.

The doctor shook off his torpor. "Driver!" he shouted, banging his stick upon the roof. "Driver, this is not the way to Covent Garden!"

The hatch opened again. "I goes a roundabout way," the cabman replied. "Avoids the traffic."

"I warn you, I shall not be cheated," Van Detta declared. "I shall report you to the authorities."

The hansom cab proceeded at a leisurely pace down Northumberland, then turned left onto the Embankment. The doctor sat forward in his seat, alert for any sort of larceny. He had to admit, though, that traffic on the Embankment was less tangled than on the other avenues. *I must remember this route in the future,* he noted.

Dr. Van Detta was just beginning to trust the cabman again, when the cab unexpectedly pulled across the Embankment traffic and stopped. They had halted near a pillar of stone known as Cleopatra's Needle. This ancient artifact, nearly seventy feet high, stood at the edge of the Embankment, flanked by a pair of bronze sphinxes and sets of stairs leading down to a pier.

"Why are you stopping?" the doctor demanded. "I shall miss the overture!"

"Horse needs water," the driver replied. Indeed, the horse was already dipping his muzzle into one of the granite water troughs set up along the Embankment.

The doctor was even more surprised when the driver hopped down from the cab and walked slowly toward the river.

"Driver! Where are you going?" Van Detta called. "What is the meaning of this? Come back here! I order you!"

The cabman disregarded the doctor's commands. Without looking back, he strode across the pavement toward the base of Cleopatra's Needle, where he descended the stairs and passed from sight.

Dr. Van Detta was mystified. Did the driver want him to follow? What if the cabman were luring him into some kind of ambush? *Criminals are always ready to prey on foreigners,* he warned himself. And then there were his rivals to consider. Perhaps one of them had arranged an unpleasant surprise. The doctor tightened his grip on his walking stick.

Despite his apprehensions, Van Detta was too curious to ignore the cabman's behavior. He stepped cautiously down from the cab. He looked around. Cabs and coaches moved up and down the street. Three loud soldiers staggered along the Embankment, bumping and shoving each other as they attempted to sing a tune none of them seemed to know—a fact that did not lessen their enjoyment in the least. A blind beggar tooting a pennywhistle sat on a bench held up by cast-iron camels. A man hurried by carrying an armload of second-hand umbrellas. Nothing seemed amiss. *Still, I had best be cautious,* the doctor thought. He removed the brass cap from the lethal end of the walking stick and slipped the cap into his pocket. Then he proceeded toward the river.

When Dr. Van Detta stepped down to the stone pier, he found the cabman alone, leaning on a railing beside the water. The doctor took a place at the railing, at a safe distance from the driver.

The two figures gazed out over the Thames, ebbing now toward the sea. The evening sun, dipping below the city's smoky haze, spilled its coppery light upon the water.

"You can barely picture the old river, the way it was before Bazalgette captured it with this Embankment," said the driver, as if to himself. "Tower Bridge, Blackwall Tunnel—we build over, under, and around the river. I suppose someday we may pave it over entirely. Or move it to Scotland. We could do it, you know. We could do almost anything."

The doctor noted that the cabman no longer spoke like a cabman. "You didn't bring me here to discuss British engineering," he said. "Who are you? What do you want?"

The cabman turned toward the doctor. Raising his right arm, he slowly removed his hat. With his left hand, he pulled the whiskers away from his face and stuffed them in his pocket. "I want to be left in peace," said Barksdale.

The doctor kept his features under control; only the slight rise of an eyebrow indicated his surprise. "I had hoped to meet you before this," he said.

"I had hoped we would never meet at all," the hound replied.

"Then why did you waylay my cab?"

"Because I hoped that, by speaking to you, I might avert a tragedy," Barksdale explained.

"I'm getting close, aren't I?" said the doctor, with a satisfied grin. "I'm making you nervous."

"If you continue your pursuit," warned the hound, "there may be terrible consequences."

"Yes, yes, indeed," the doctor replied. "There may be terrible consequences. But for whom, Mr. Barksdale? That is the question."

The hound growled with annoyance. "I am not here to banter with you, Doctor. I am here to appeal to your good sense, as one gentleman to another."

"As one gentleman to another, I take very little interest in what you have to say," the doctor snapped. "And I promise you, I am not about to place my trust in a creature such as you."

Barksdale growled once more and turned his face back toward the river. After a moment, he spoke again.

"I will neither excuse nor deny the terrible crimes committed by others of my race," said the hound, as he watched a seagull fluttering like a kite over Waterloo Bridge. "But what are my crimes, Doctor? Why are you stalking me?"

"Because you are a vampire," the doctor answered matter-of-factly. "And I am in the business of vampire hunting."

"I am part vampire."

Van Detta shrugged. "In my experience, the part infects the whole. It makes you no less a monster. It makes no difference to me."

"I give you my word, Doctor: I have never infected anyone else with the vampire disease. Nor will I in the future. When I die, my family's curse will die with me."

"Very noble of you," the doctor remarked. "But a monster that can change its shape can easily change its mind."

"Then you know nothing about me," said the hound.

"I know everything about you," Van Detta shot back. "I have a doctorate in vampirology from the University of Bucharest. I have studied vampires all my life. And I know that there is only one way to deal with vampires: they must be eradicated, once and for all."

Barksdale clenched his fists. "So I am to be killed," he said, "not for doing wrong, but for being who I am."

The doctor raised his hands in a gesture of helplessness. "You were born of an evil race, sir. That is your misfortune. Blame your parents, not me."

"A respectable man would not take up your profession," charged the hound.

"Respectable!" said Van Detta. "I never hoped to be respectable, Mr. Barksdale. I was born poor. In this world, when you are born poor, you forfeit your right to respect. But I still have the right to make a living. As for the work I do, well, at least my victims are deserving, unlike the thousands of innocents you and your kind have preyed upon."

"You are the monster here," Barksdale countered.

The doctor's face grew rigid. He seemed about to rush at the hound. But in the next instant, his features softened. He laughed quietly. "Go ahead—try all of your arguments, vampire. The world sides with me, and you know it."

"I had hoped you were a man of reason," said Barksdale.

"I have reason enough to destroy you," the doctor answered. "That is all I need."

There is no argument against such animosity. It stuns the reasonable mind like a hammer blow, as it now stunned the hound. For several long moments, he regarded the doctor in silence. Finally, he sighed and placed the hat back on his head. "I am sorry to have wasted our time," Barksdale said. "If you hail a cab now, you may yet see your opera. I hear it is excellent. Good evening, Doctor."

"Stay where you are," Van Detta ordered.

Barksdale hesitated. "We have nothing further to discuss," he concluded. "Good evening." He turned to walk away.

"I said stay where you are!" With surprising nimbleness, the doctor cut in front of the hound, blocking his retreat.

"What is the meaning of this?" asked Barksdale.

Van Detta raised his walking stick until the point was a foot from the hound's muzzle.

"I am unarmed, sir," said Barksdale.

"Oh, but you have your vampire powers," the doctor countered. "That makes you quite dangerous enough. Did you really think, after all the time I have spent hunting you, that I would simply allow you to walk away?" Edging forward, he backed the hound against the base of the obelisk.

"I had hoped we would part on better terms," said Barksdale. "But I was prepared, either way."

"Let us see how well you have prepared," Van Detta replied. He took a fencer's stance, his left arm curled behind him, his right arm waving the stick at Barksdale.

The hound made no move but bared his teeth. "I should warn you, Doctor: when I came here, I had no intention of harming you, but I will defend myself."

"Then do it," the doctor replied. He stepped in, stabbing at Barksdale with the stick. The hound swatted the blow aside with his left forearm. Again the doctor thrust at Barksdale's chest. There was a metallic clang. The hound grunted and staggered backward against the monument.

"What the devil was that?" Van Detta demanded, lowering his weapon.

"I told you I was prepared either way," Barksdale answered.

The doctor nodded. "I see. You are unarmed but not unarmored. Very well."

Van Detta dropped the stick to the ground. He removed his hat, placing it on the ground beside the stick. He took off his gloves, dropping them into the hat. Then he slowly removed his coat.

"What are you doing?" asked Barksdale.

"Do you know how I escaped from the slums of Amsterdam?" the doctor responded, beginning to roll up his sleeves. "Do you know how I paid for my education? With my fists, sir. Boxing.

That is how I received this crease upon my nose. That is how I won these pretty knuckles." He showed the hound his right fist. The knuckles were like barnacles, large and misshapen. "If I cannot use a weapon against you, I will have to make do with bare hands."

The doctor now assumed a boxing pose.

The hound removed his gloves. He held up his paws, so Van Detta might see his claws. They were long again; he had allowed them to grow back, just in case.

"I'm not afraid of you," the doctor boasted.

"I would rather not do this," said Barksdale. He tapped his chest with a claw. "You'll break your fists, sir."

"I'll break your skull first," Van Detta replied. "Now, box."

The doctor and the hound began circling each other. Jab! Jab! Jab! The doctor's left fist searched for Barksdale's face, but the hound parried the blows. Van Detta swung with his right. The hound dodged, and slashed with his own right. The doctor's head snapped back. He raised his hand to his cheek. There was blood on his fingertips.

He saw Barksdale's eyes grow wide. "You can't resist it, can you?" said Van Detta, holding up his bloody hand. "So much for your fine promises."

Embarrassment flamed in Barksdale's face, followed swiftly by anger rumbling deep in his throat. "You don't know me," the hound said.

The doctor resumed sparring. He feinted a punch at the hound's head, then suddenly bent low, lashing out with his right leg. His whipping boot caught the hound beneath the knees, sweeping Barksdale off his feet. The hound fell heavily to the pavement. In an instant the doctor was on top of him, pinning Barksdale's arms.

Both fighters were breathing hard. "No shape-changing?" said Van Detta, pressing his blood-smeared face close to the hound. "No disappearing in a puff of smoke? You are a poor sort of vampire, Mr. Barksdale."

The hound snarled, displaying all of his pointed teeth.

"Yet you still have the bite, don't you?" the doctor taunted. "The bite you say you would never use. Are you wishing you could use it now?"

The hound snarled again and opened his jaws. *Do it!* Barksdale thought. *Use the bite! Protect yourself! Protect Potts!* He craned his neck, stretching out toward the doctor's throat. He opened his jaws wider . . .

. . . And snapped them shut on nothing but air. His head sank back on the ground. The cruel teeth disappeared behind his lips. His heart was beating against his ribs.

"Whatever I am, I am a creature of my word," said Barksdale.

"I'm glad to hear it," the doctor gloated, "as that will make destroying you all the easier. Let us see what it will take."

Van Detta shifted his weight. He pinned Barksdale's left arm under his knee, thereby freeing his own right hand, which he wrapped around the hound's throat. He began to squeeze.

Barksdale struggled. Arching his back, he twisted frantically from side to side, desperately trying to throw the doctor off.

Van Detta's grip grew tighter. The hound became more frantic.

And then, before either of the combatants was aware of what was happening, a pair of hands were pulling the doctor away and a gruff voice was saying, "Here now! What's this? That's enough, the both of you!"

The bobby was tall and heavyset, the strap of his domed helmet cutting into his fleshy chin. He yanked Van Detta to his feet. Placing a hand firmly in the middle of the doctor's chest, he pushed the man away from the hound.

"We takes a dim view of gentlemen brawling in public," the bobby said, glaring at the doctor. "If you two has differences, I suggest you settle 'em in private, else you'll be spending the rest of the night in jail. Is that understood?"

"It's quite clear," said Van Detta, with disgust. "Though I'm afraid my opponent was not listening."

The bobby turned around. "Hey! Where'd he go to?" he exclaimed. Rushing to the railing, the bobby searched the water below for any sign of the hound. But he saw no one in the river. He ran up and down the stairs, circling the base of the obelisk. He scanned the Embankment in both directions. There was no sign of Barksdale.

"Never seen anyone disappear like that," said the bobby, shaking his head.

"Perhaps he flew away," the doctor suggested.

"Don't talk smart to me," the bobby warned, placing a hand on the truncheon hanging from his belt. "I better not catch you or your friend down here again. Now, shove off, before I has you up before a magistrate."

While the policeman stared, the doctor slowly put on his hat, coat, and gloves. With equal ease, he retrieved his walking stick. Then, tipping his hat to the bobby, Dr. Van Detta turned and walked back toward the Embankment to hail another cab.

Cleopatra's Needle was a stone obelisk from the ancient city of Heliopolis in Egypt. Despite its name, the obelisk had nothing to do with Cleopatra, having been carved nearly one thousand five hundred years before the reign of that famous Egyptian queen. It had been presented to Britain by the Turkish governor of Egypt in 1819. The journey to England had been long and perilous, however, and it was not until 1878 that the obelisk had been set in place on the Embankment. There Londoners could marvel at the beautiful and mysterious Egyptian hieroglyphs covering all four sides of the pink granite pillar. On that particular evening, however, the hieroglyphs were not the only interesting feature of the monument. For a short time that night, a black-clad canine stood boldly upon the summit of Cleopatra's Needle, like Lord

Nelson atop his column in Trafalgar Square; and, like Lord Nelson, he seemed to be contemplating the destruction of his enemies.

"Were you successful, sir?" asked Tilney, when his master returned. He helped Barksdale out of his coat. The rat's whiskers twitched with alarm when he saw the hole in the left side and the spot of blood on the lapel.

"I'm afraid not," Barksdale replied wearily. "The doctor is not a man to be put off by arguments." The hound removed his shirt, revealing a silver breastplate. There was a small scratch over the heart, where Dr. Van Detta had tried to stab him.

"It was good you were prepared, sir," said Tilney, unfastening the buckles on the breastplate.

"I am grateful for your suggestion, Potts. By the way, where did you get this piece of armor?"

"My Uncle Jarvis works at the British Museum, sir."

"Good heavens, Potts!" said the hound. "You don't mean to tell me this piece is from the museum's collection? And now I've scratched it!"

"I wouldn't worry, sir," soothed the rat. "A little silver polish and it will be good as new. It was worth it to preserve your life."

"I suppose you are right, Potts. Still . . ."

"And besides, sir," Tilney added, "I don't think Julius Caesar will be needing it anytime soon."

X

The Gentlemen of the Committee

Two days later, Slatkin and Chuggers were summoned to a meeting with the doctor in St. James's Park. They found him seated on a bench near the lake.

"Looks like you've had an accident," said Slatkin, noting the doctor's bandaged cheek.

"It's nothing," Van Detta replied, turning his wound away from the ferret. "A scratch from a low-hanging branch."

"A tree branch, hey? I was afraid some tough give you one on the cheek. Or maybe some vampire sunk—"

"I told you," said the doctor icily. "It is nothing."

"Anyways, I hope you'll soon be on the mend," Slatkin sympathized.

"Your concern is a great comfort to me," said the doctor sourly.

"I bashed my mug into a tree once," Chuggers told them. "I were running from the constables on Hampstead Heath—"

"Anything to report?" the doctor interrupted.

"—and I brushes a branch, and this squirrel falls on my head," Chuggers continued. "Now, he has his tail over my good eye, so I can't see nothing, but the constables is—"

"Anything to report?" the doctor repeated, with increased irritation.

"And I ran into a tree, but I got away," the bear concluded hastily.

There was enough room for all on the park bench, but Van Detta had not invited the bear and the ferret to sit down—a fact that was readily apparent to all three of them. So Slatkin and Chuggers stood, scuffing their boots and looking at each other as if they couldn't decide what to say next.

"Out with it," the doctor ordered.

"It were last Wednesday," Slatkin began. "Chuggers and me were on the job—we is always on the job, you see, sir—when we happened to spot the little rat coming along New Oxford Street. So we decides to follow him, reckoning he'd lead us to the vampire's home."

"Excellent," said the doctor. "What happened?"

"So we follows him, real sly-like, so he don't have any idea we is on his tail."

"But he don't have no tail," Chuggers corrected him.

"Will you let me tell it?" said Slatkin.

"Then tell it right," Chuggers replied.

"I am telling it right!"

"Then you oughtn't to be putting tails in where there ain't none," the bear insisted.

"What happened?" asked the doctor.

"Then he went into a ladies' shop on Oxford Street," the ferret said.

"And?"

Slatkin looked at Chuggers. "And then we lost him."

"Lost him!" The doctor jumped to his feet. "You idiots! How could you lose him?"

The bear and the ferret pulled in their necks and tucked their arms close to their sides, trying to look as small and guiltless as possible.

"He went out a back door which Slatkin said weren't there," Chuggers explained.

"There weren't no back door!" the ferret countered. "We lost him because you was too busy eating carrots to watch the front door!"

"Oh, and who ate the last carrot?" argued Chuggers, waving a fist at the ferret. "I seen you pinch the last one while my back was turned."

"I never!" Slatkin objected.

"Enough!" shouted the doctor. "Cease this bickering right now or, I swear, I will turn you both into rugs for my drawing room."

That ended the argument.

"Why was the rat in the ladies' shop?" Van Detta asked.

The partners shrugged. "When we tried to question the shopgirl," the ferret related, "she yells, 'Go back across the Channel where you belongs!' Then she runs into the street, hollering for someone to save her from 'the Frenchmen.' We had to beat it out of there double-quick."

"I been called a lot of nasty things in my day," Chuggers declared, "but I never been called a Frenchman."

The doctor stroked his bandaged cheek and watched the pigeons strutting around the bench. "The rat is the key to the puzzle," he stated, after a time. "You saw him on the street. He must deal with tradesmen. He must run errands for his master. Someone must know him. Someone must know his habits. Bring me the servant, and we will soon have the master. Go back to Oxford Street. Go to New Oxford Street. Talk to everyone. Find the rat. Start now."

Slatkin and Chuggers saluted the doctor and marched away. They returned to Oxford Street, united in their resolve to locate the rat, though still divided on the question of who ate the last carrot.

Despite their increased diligence, Slatkin and Chuggers were not immediately able to uncover more information about Tilney Potts. This was due to the fact that, through years of practice, Tilney had developed very discreet shopping habits. He rarely dealt with the tradesmen near Harker Lane, often going far out of his way to shop in Chelsea or Notting Hill. Certain items, such as Mr. Barksdale's suits and shirts, were ordered from a tailor in Bond Street through Mr. Church, the hound's trusted solicitor, who oversaw all of Barksdale's accounts, as well as his correspondence. The result was that, although Tilney was sometimes seen in the neighborhood of Oxford Street, he wasn't well-known.

Slatkin and Chuggers questioned numerous tradesmen, none of whom seemed eager to chat with the shabby "detectives." The response was always the same: a puzzled frown, then a shake of the head. Repeated failure discouraged the ferret and the bear, but it did not stop them. They were eager to find the rat, if only to rid themselves of Dr. Van Detta forever. They worked their way eastward along Oxford Street, to New Oxford Street, then High Holborn, with frequent fruitless detours into Soho, Bloomsbury, or St. Giles. Finally, they crossed Holborn Viaduct. They passed near Newgate Prison, which made both of them shudder. And then, in a tea shop on Bread Street, they finally had some luck. They met a Mrs. Jenkins, who said that, as she recollected, Nan Hodge had a brother who had lost his tail in an accident on a coal barge. Nan had sewn the dress Mrs. Jenkins was wearing. Very becoming, Slatkin had said, just the kind of thing he wanted for his own missus. Did Mrs. Hodge reside in the neighborhood? As luck would have it, she lived not five minutes away.

Fred Hodge bent over the scrap of paper, his eyebrows joined in concentration. He sketched a few shapes on the paper, held the drawing up in front of him, and frowned. "I don't know," he said. "Seems like Liza could draw Her Majesty just as well.

Maybe I ain't the artist for the job." He wanted to show the sketch to Molly, but the girl was absent, having cajoled her father into allowing her a short walk toward Ludgate Hill to relieve the tedium of the cheese shop.

At that moment, the shop door opened, and two customers entered. Fred set the paper down on the counter.

"What can I do for you gents?" asked Fred.

"I'd like a ha'penny of cheese, if you would," said the ferret.

"I'd like more than that," added the ferret's companion, a seedy one-eyed bear.

"Has you got the money for it?" the ferret replied sharply.

"You know you has all the money," the bear countered.

"And I say we gets a ha'penny's worth," the ferret concluded, with a finality that ended the discussion.

"What kind of cheese would you like?" Fred inquired, showing the customers his meager stock. "Cheddar? Cheshire? Or I has some very fine double Gloucester."

"I'll have the Cheddar," said the ferret.

"Cheshire," the bear corrected him.

The ferret stared hard at the bear. He turned to Fred. "All right, Cheshire," he said.

Fred sliced the cheese, weighed it, and wrapped the thin wedge in a piece of newspaper. The ferret handed him the halfpenny. Fred started to pass him the cheese, but the bear's hefty paw intercepted it.

"Anything else, gents?" asked Fred.

"Not today, thanks," said the ferret. He started toward the door, then stopped and placed his paw to his chin, as if he had just remembered something. "Unless," said the ferret. "Unless you knows a rat name of Fred Hodge."

"Well, I knows that name as well as my own," Fred answered, "because it is my own."

"You don't say!" exclaimed the ferret, gaping with amazement. "And is you also the Fred Hodge who has a wife named Nan?"

"I am," said Fred.

"And is your Nan the Nan who was formerly Nan Potts, which has a brother named Tilney Potts?"

"I am," Fred repeated. "I mean, she is, she has."

The ferret gave the bear a sly look of triumph. "Well, then, this is a most fortunate coincidence," said the ferret, with a smile. "Allow me to introduce myself. I am Mr. Wilkes, and this is my friend, Mr. Tingle." They all shook paws.

"What's this about my Nan and her brother?" Fred inquired.

"You see," the ferret explained, "we happen to be members of the Citizens' Committee for the Queen's Diamond Jubilee."

"You don't look like committee men," Fred cut in, noting the threadbare clothing worn by the two customers.

"Too true, too true. You has a keen eye, Mr. Hodge," the ferret replied. He leaned across the counter, placing his paw beside his mouth. "To be honest, friend, we has mostly joined the committee to partake of a little free food and drink at the monthly meetings. No harm in a couple o' working blokes dining like gentlemen for an evening, is there?" He winked at Fred.

"I still don't see what this has to do with my Nan," said Fred.

"Our committee," the ferret continued, "has been charged with finding the very best personages from all stations to represent the citizens of London in the Queen's Diamond Jubilee celebration. It just so happens that your wife's brother, Mr. Tilney Potts, has been recommended as a representative from the serving class."

"Well, I see," said Fred. "Good for Tilney."

"There is only one problem," the ferret went on, shaking his head.

"What's that?" asked Fred.

"We has been unable to locate Mr. Potts to inform him of this high honor. Some paperwork bungle, I suppose. But, as you is related, perhaps you can tell us where we may find him." The ferret and the bear looked eagerly at Fred.

Fred scratched his jaw. "I'm afraid I can't be much help," he said.

Disappointment showed on the faces of his audience. "Why's that?" asked the bear.

"Tilney is terrible closemouthed about his employer," Fred complained. "I don't know where his employer lives, nor even his name."

"No clue at all?" asked the ferret.

"All I knows is what I hears from my kids. They say Tilney's employer is as rich as a maharaja. House full of rubies and elephants and all. And some story about a pet snake."

"Don't like snakes," the bear muttered.

"Sounds like a regular zoo," said the ferret. "Does Mr. Potts sometimes visit with the children then?"

"Comes to tea every other Wednesday," said Fred. A light went on in Fred's eyes. "He comes to tea every other Wednesday!" he repeated, slapping the counter. "He'll be here tomorrow!"

"What luck!" the ferret exclaimed. "So, if we was to drop by at teatime, just for a minute, so as not to intrude, we might inform him of the committee's decision?"

"I don't see why not," Fred replied.

"Very good," said the ferret, offering Fred his paw. "You has been most helpful. Oh, and if you would," he continued, lowering his voice, "don't breathe a word of this to your wife or Mr. Potts. Surprise makes the honor all the more exciting, don't you see?"

Fred agreed to keep the conversation a secret.

"Good day to you, then," said the ferret, turning toward the door.

"Just a minute, gents," Fred called.

"Yes?" the ferret replied, with a nervous glance at the bear. "We really must be going. Committee business, you know."

"I was thinking," said Fred, "well, hardly thinking—just

toying with the idea, really—that I might perhaps carve a bust of Her Majesty out of cheese. To present to her, perhaps, at her jubilee. Does that sound like a good idea to you?"

"What kind of cheese?" asked the bear.

"Well, Cheddar, I suppose," said Fred.

"I likes Cheshire," said the bear.

"I'm certain that Her Majesty would deeply appreciate any kind of cheese sculpture," the ferret concluded hastily. "Good luck to you, Mr. Hodge." He and the bear exited the shop.

Fred was leaning on the counter, lost in thought, when Nan entered from the back room.

"Fred Hodge, what is you thinking?" asked Nan, noting her husband's dreamy look.

"Now, Nan," Fred replied, "you know I never does no thinking."

Slatkin and Chuggers hurried away from Fred Hodge's cheese shop.

"So now we knows when and where to find the little rat," the ferret gloated, swaggering with satisfaction. "We should tell the doctor right quick. Don't suppose he'd favor us with a bonus, do you think?"

"I thought we had committee business to attend to," said Chuggers.

"What committee?" Slatkin asked.

"The Queen's jubilee committee," said Chuggers, "which I never heared nothing about until today, even though we is partners. How many of them meetings has you been to without me?"

The ferret rolled his eyes. "There ain't no committee," he said.

"Sure there ain't," answered the bear. "And I suppose there ain't no queen, neither."

"What are you talking about?" Slatkin demanded. "'Course there's a queen."

"Which is just my point," Chuggers replied, halting on the pavement.

"You ain't got a point," was Slatkin's retort. "You ain't had a point since the day you was born, and you ain't going to get one now."

"All right, then, don't tell me about your committee," Chuggers said. He poked a thick finger into the ferret's narrow chest. "I'll find out about the next meeting and go myself. Ain't going to let you hog all the free food. Some friend you is." Muttering and waving his paws, the bear stomped off in the opposite direction.

The ferret ground his teeth in anger and exasperation. "I hope you finds your meeting!" he called after the bear. "I hope you finds it in China!"

Slatkin shoved his paws in his pockets and resumed his walk. *Just like him to make a mess of a good thing,* the ferret thought. *Here we finally gets a break in our case, and that fleabag has to go off chasing nothing. You can't make a sensible explanation to someone who has got no sense. I know one thing: if ever I gets on a committee, my first motion is that we exclude all bears what has got no brains.*

Suddenly, the ferret froze in mid-stride. "Blast it all!" he cried, stamping his foot. "That bear has got no brains, but he has got all the cheese! Blast it all!"

He quickly whirled around. "Chuggers!" he hollered. "Chuuuuggers!"

Too late. The bear was out of earshot.

"Him and his one good ear," Slatkin griped. "Probably wouldn't hear me, even if he could hear me. Blast it all."

The ferret kept walking. Farther along the street, he halted to watch a group of ragged children dancing on the pavement to the music of an organ-grinder. Slatkin was amazed at the way these little scarecrows could hop and twirl and prance as prettily as any music hall performer he had ever seen. *How can they be so light and quick,* he wondered, *when life is every day weighing them down?*

"They is all little pixies, ain't they?" the organ-grinder yelled above the music. He had a pockmarked face and a gray mustache that hung like icicles from his upper lip.

A dark-haired girl of about five, clad in a dress from which every bit of color had faded, stopped her whirling and smiled at the ferret.

Slatkin returned the smile and doffed his hat. "May I have this dance, little miss?" he asked, extending his paw.

The girl shyly took Slatkin's paw. They danced. As the organ-grinder cranked away, the urchin leaped from one bare foot to another, curling and snapping like a ribbon in a gale, while the ferret shuffled around her, barely hanging on to the girl's thin fingers.

Finally, the organ-grinder ended the tune. Coughing and wheezing, Slatkin bowed to his partner. "Thank you, miss," he gasped. "You dances like a princess."

The girl blushed and covered her face with her hands. With a happy squeal, she ran away, disappearing around the corner.

"You is a might' fine dancer, guvnuh," said the organ-grinder to Slatkin. "Ought to be in the ballet." He held out a tin cup toward the ferret. "A copper for the entertainment?"

Slatkin wiped his face with his handkerchief. "Sorry, mate," he answered. "My purse is as light as my head."

"Off you go then," the organ-grinder said curtly. Turning his back on Slatkin, he began cranking out another tune. The ferret went on his way.

As Slatkin was crossing the Holborn Viaduct, a wagon pulled to a halt beside him. Two large, tough-looking men hopped down from the seat. They planted themselves on the pavement in front of Slatkin, blocking the ferret's way.

"What do you want?" said Slatkin.

"You Slatkin?" asked one of the men, pointing a finger at the ferret. Slatkin caught a glimpse of a green snake tattooed on the man's right forearm.

"That's him all right," said the other man, opening his coat just wide enough so Slatkin could see the handle of a knife protruding from his belt. "Come on," the man with the knife said to the ferret. "Into the wagon. Let's go."

"Where am I going?" Slatkin asked, without moving.

"Toby wants to see yer," the tattooed man replied.

Toby! Slatkin thought. *This is no time for Toby!*

"What does Toby want with me?" the ferret inquired, though he knew very well what Toby wanted.

The man with the knife moved his hand to the hilt. "He don't tell us," he said. "He wants to tell you. Now, does you want to get in the wagon whole or in bits? It makes no difference to me."

Slatkin's eyes darted around the street, searching for any means of escape or rescue. Why was there never a bobby nearby when a bloke was really in trouble? Aha! Wouldn't you know? There was one now, and he was heading their way!

A short constable with the build of a marble block marched purposefully across the street toward Slatkin and the two thugs.

"Everything all right here?" the constable asked. He stood with his legs wide apart, rocking slightly on his heels.

The thug with the knife had quickly closed his coat as the bobby approached. Now he said, "No trouble here, constable. Merely collecting a parcel for Mr. Toby Thigpen." As he said the name, he gave the bobby a knowing look.

Whether the bobby returned the look or not, it was impossible for Slatkin to say, for the constable wore his helmet so low over his eyes that he must have seen London only from the pavement to the knees. In any case, he replied, "Mr. Toby Thigpen, eh? Well, you be sure to give Mr. Thigpen my compliments."

Before Slatkin could object, the constable had turned his back on the thugs, who grabbed the ferret by the arms and heaved him onto the wagon.

XI

Sticky Business

Slatkin sat wedged between his two captors as the wagon rolled across Southwark Bridge. Given any room at all, he would have bolted from the seat and flung himself into the Thames. Though he wasn't a good swimmer, the ferret reasoned that gulping dirty river water might be preferable to another interview with Toby Thigpen.

It was all about the money, of course. With Toby, it was always about money. It had begun with a sovereign that Slatkin had been forced to borrow in order to pay off a police inspector. This inspector was going to arrest the ferret for a burglary in Chelsea, even though Slatkin was innocent of the charge, having spent the night in question trying—without success—to break into a home in Mayfair. Obviously, Slatkin couldn't use that as an alibi, so he had no choice but to pay up. Toby had been happy to lend him the cash—at considerable interest, of course. But then Slatkin hadn't been able to pay the money back, and the debt had grown. The ferret now owed Toby three pounds, five shillings, and sixpence. It wasn't a particularly large sum, but it was more money than Slatkin could ever hope to scrape together. In any case, the size of the debt hardly mattered. All sums, large and small, were important to Toby. That's why he was a prosperous pig.

London south of the Thames was a jumble of docks, warehouses, and decaying neighborhoods, all of them caught in the iron coils of the city's southern rail lines. Noisy, grim-faced factories churned out pottery, glass, soap, candles, hats, leather, glue, beer, and countless other products. The landscape festered with reeking factory ponds and polluted streams. It was a region of strong smells, from the sugary aroma of jam to the acrid mustiness of animal hides cured in dog dung.

The wagon rattled through Bermondsey, finally stopping outside a grimy brick building bearing a faded sign that read IMPERIAL GLUE COMPANY. The stench seeping through the cracked and broken windows of the factory burned the ferret's nose and throat and made his eyes water.

"How . . . can you . . . stand it?" asked Slatkin, between coughs. He covered the lower half of his face with his paws.

"You gets used to it," said the man with the tattoo. "At first, it give me awful headaches. But now I don't even notice it no more."

"Yeah, now this here place smells just like Kew Gardens, don't it?" the other man commented, and they both laughed.

The two thugs escorted Slatkin inside. London's glue factories were the receptacles for all the waste that poured out of the slaughterhouses, tanneries, and meat processing plants of the great city. Slatkin's nose wrinkled in disgust at the sight of washing tubs filled with ears, tails, scraps of hides, tendons, bones, and feet.

Hope that ain't anyone I know, the ferret thought. *Hope it ain't about to be me!*

The floors were so slick with animal fat that Slatkin felt as if he were skating. Losing his balance, he grabbed the arm of the tattooed thug.

"Give off, ya stinkin' weasel," the thug growled, pushing Slatkin away.

The ferret passed large vats where lime was mixed with the

animal hides, causing the skins to swell and break down. He saw haggard, sweaty men with long wooden paddles stirring cauldrons of boiling animal remains. This boiling would produce collagen, the brown, sticky substance that made the glue used by all the furniture makers of London. It was clear to Slatkin that someone—such as himself—could walk into Toby's factory and wind up stuck to the legs of a table in a furniture shop on Tottenham Court Road.

The factory workers didn't look up from their work as the ferret and his guards passed by; they had learned that it was best not to notice certain things about Mr. Thigpen's business. Had anyone asked them, however, they might have said that they envied the ferret, whatever his trouble, simply because he was not forced to spend his days in a glue factory.

At the rear of the factory, tucked behind walls of packing cases containing glue pots, was an office room on a raised platform. The tattooed man shoved Slatkin up the stairs and into the office, then shut the door behind the ferret. The two thugs remained on guard outside.

"Blimey," said Slatkin, looking around. Rather than the usual hodgepodge of desks, chairs, bookcases, stools, ledgers, and inkwells, the office contained only a dining room table draped in a white tablecloth. A silver candelabrum—its six tapers struggling to pull oxygen out of the stifling air—stood upon the tablecloth, while at one end of the table—in a high-backed wooden chair, elaborately carved with griffins, stars, and ivy, so that it resembled a throne more than a chair—sat Toby Thigpen, a white napkin tied under his chins.

"Well, if it isn't my good friend Slatkin," said the pig, with his mouth full of food. The fat old boar bent his thick snout close to his dinner tray. The ferret could see the well-oiled bristles on his scalp shining in the candlelight.

"You'd care to join me, maybe?" Toby asked, between bites. With a greasy trotter, he tipped up the dinner tray for the ferret to see. The pig's dinner consisted of fruit rinds, fish heads, brown and blackened vegetables, and meat scraps a butcher wouldn't throw to his dog.

"No thanks, Toby," said Slatkin, trying not to look ill. "I guess I ain't that hungry."

"He guesses he ain't that hungry!" Toby replied, laughing and spitting potato skin onto the tablecloth. "Did you hear that, Jack? He's different from you. You'll eat anything, won't you, Jack? Never saw a free meal you didn't like."

A large raven flew down from the rafters, landing on the table with a heavy thump that nearly toppled the candelabrum.

"Be careful, Jack!" cried Toby. "You want to start the Great Fire of London all over again?"

"Sorry, boss," said the raven, in a raspy voice. "Sorry, sorry."

The raven cocked his head, fixing one of his dark eyes on Slatkin. His long thin beak curled into a sneer. "Ferret's back, boss," he said. "Filthy ferret. He owes, boss. Filthy ferret owes."

"Now, now, Jack," the pig cautioned, as he stuffed a rotten apple in his cheek, "there's no need to be rude to a customer. Besides, maybe Mr. Slatkin has come to make a payment on his account. What does he owe us today, Jack?"

"Three pounds, five and six," snapped the bird. "Overdue."

"See why I employ this remarkable fellow?" Toby said to Slatkin. "He keeps all my accounts right there in his little feathered head. Anything I want to know about my money, I just have to ask Jack. Saves me a fortune in ledgers and clerks, I tell you. Keeping it all straight, Jack?"

"Straight, boss," the raven replied. "Straight, straight."

"Good," said Toby, with a smile. The bits of food trapped between his rotten teeth looked like rubbish caught against a splintered fence. "Because if I thought the figures were getting crooked, Jack, I might have to straighten you out on a cooking spit."

"It's straight, boss," the raven repeated crossly.

"Now, Mr. Slatkin," said Toby, "you have heard Jack refer to the amount in question. Maybe you have some money to pay me? A few coins, perhaps, to make old Toby feel more kindly toward the world in general and you in particular?"

The ferret shrugged. "Afraid not, Toby. I'm broke, you see."

"Skin him, boss. Skin him," hissed the raven.

Slatkin tried to toast the bird with his stare.

The pig shook his head sadly. "I am sorry to hear of your predicament, ferret. These are hard times indeed. Hard times for all of us. Do you know how much I pay in bribes every month? You can't imagine. Why, I hand over one hundred and thirty-six pounds to the peelers alone."

"Hundred thirty-two pounds," the raven corrected him.

"Really, Jack?"

"Constable Lewis. Turned honest," the raven reported.

The pig frowned. "That's the problem with policemen—you can't trust them to be crooked."

Slatkin yawned loudly.

"Oh, dear, are we boring you?" asked Toby.

"Not at all, Toby," answered Slatkin, looking bored. "I musta been yawning with excitement."

"I do apologize," said the pig. "Finance can be so tedious. If I had to work in a bank, I should be as bored as . . . as . . . a board!" He laughed, spraying the raven with apple bits.

"Good joke, boss," muttered Jack. He wiped his face with his wing.

Toby's expression suddenly turned serious. "But you have no money for me today?" he asked the ferret once more.

"Like I said," Slatkin replied.

"Nothing for me, your old friend? Your benefactor? Toby-who-kept-you-out-of-prison? And yet you have coins to spare for little beggars in public cemeteries."

"Says who?"

"Eyes and ears, ferret. Eyes and ears. I have hundreds of

them, all over London. A Guardsman at the palace doesn't blink without my knowing about it."

"If you know so much," the ferret challenged, "then why don't you find this bloke I been searching for and save me the trouble? You must know where he is."

"Maybe I could find him—"

"You could, boss. You could," the raven interrupted.

"Thank you, Jack. Maybe I could find him, Slatkin. Maybe I could have found Dr. Livingstone in deepest Africa. But, you see, I'm not in the finding business. I'm not opposed to making someone disappear now and then, maybe. But finding? No, that's not my business. That is your business at present. Any luck?"

"Maybe," said Slatkin, looking the pig in the eye.

"Skin him, boss. Skin him!" screeched the raven.

Snatching an apple core from his platter, Toby bounced it off the raven's head. The black bird wobbled, then keeled over onto the tablecloth.

"Ha! I surprised you with that one, Jack!" the pig declared. "What a shot! Not as good as last week, though," Toby told Slatkin. "Last week I got him while he was on the wing. Hit him with a walnut at twenty paces. He dropped like a stone."

"Congratulations," the ferret replied. "I only wish I'd done it myself."

The raven lay on his back, twitching his wings and legs, while uttering small, pitiful cries.

"Oh, stop being so dramatic!" Toby ordered. "Get up, before I replace you with a pigeon."

The raven hopped back on his feet. "That hurt, boss," he complained. "It hurt."

"I'll make it up to you, Jack," the pig promised. He turned his attention back to Slatkin. "Ferret, I suggest you conclude your business with the doctor as quickly as possible, so that you may receive your due, whereupon I may receive your due. You see my meaning?"

Slatkin nodded.

"Because if I don't receive full payment in one week, I will double your debt. Won't I, Jack?"

"You will, boss. You will."

"That ain't fair," Slatkin objected.

"Fair does not enter into it," the pig explained. "This isn't football; this is business."

"Business, boss," croaked the raven.

"It's a crime 's what it is," Slatkin fumed. "And you ain't nothing but a rubbish-eating old boar, no matter what kind of fancy table you sets!"

"Rubbish!" shrieked the raven. "Rubbish, he says, boss!"

"Calm yourself, Jack," said the pig. "Though he thinks to insult me, our friend has merely spoken the truth. Yes, ferret, I do eat rubbish." He selected a moldy strawberry from the platter and popped it into his mouth. "I dine on what respectable people would never touch. And so I have all I can eat for free, while you empty your pockets to buy a few crumbs. Who has the better deal, maybe? Could it be me?"

"You can have your rubbish," muttered Slatkin. "I hope it chokes you."

Toby grunted. "I'm afraid this is not proper dinner conversation. Jack, would you like to peck our ferret friend out of the building?"

Before Slatkin could even open his mouth to protest, the raven attacked. The evil bird hurled itself at the ferret's head, beating him with its large black wings, raking his face with its claws, pecking at his skull with its sharp beak. Slatkin ducked his head and flailed his arms, desperately trying to fend off the assault. He backed toward the office door and threw it open. The raven rushed him again, and Slatkin tumbled down the stairs, much to the delight of the two thugs waiting outside.

Scrambling to his feet, the ferret hunched over, covering his head with his paws as he ran through the factory. The raven pursued him like a swarm of hornets. Again and again the bird's cruel beak tore at the ferret's paws, so that Slatkin's yelps of pain mingled with the screeching of the raven and the mocking laughter of Toby and his henchmen.

Slatkin slipped and fell hard on the greasy floor. His hat rolled away. He crawled after it and shoved it back on his head.

It ain't right, Slatkin thought. *It ain't fair.*

"Out! Out, dirty ferret!" screamed the bird, pouncing on him. Striking out with his fists, the ferret fought his way back onto his feet.

Slatkin's stumbling retreat took him past the bubbling vats. He noticed one of the long wooden paddles standing idle beside a cauldron. In desperation, he snatched it up. He swung the paddle wildly about his head. On the second swing, he connected. With a squawk of surprise, Jack made a long, fluttering arc through the air, like a black shuttlecock, until he landed— plop!—in a vat of glue.

"Oh! Help! Oh, I'll get you!" shrieked the raven, as he squirmed and flopped in the sticky morass. "Save me! Get him!"

The factory workers stopped their toil and shook with suppressed laughter.

"Well struck, ferret!" Toby Thigpen roared. "Looks like maybe you're stuck, Jack! Looks like maybe your goose is cooked!"

"Get me out, boss! Get me out!" the raven screamed.

Slatkin did not stay to see if Jack was rescued. He threw the paddle to the floor and sprinted out of the factory. He ran as hard as he could toward the river, until the foul air set his lungs to boiling, forcing him to stop. He clung to a hitching post, coughing as though his heart would come out his throat.

After a while, the coughs were less convulsive. The ferret straightened up. He drew three long, slow breaths. He spat several times, then wiped his face with his kerchief.

"Slatkin, there is two kinds of people in this town," he gasped, "and you always seems to know the wrong kind."

XII

Missing

The drawing room clock began to chime. Barksdale looked up from his book. Six o'clock. He cocked an ear. The house seemed perfectly still, except for the clock. No footsteps in the hall. No rattling from the kitchen downstairs. Where in the world was Potts?

"Oh, yes," Barksdale said. It was the fourth Wednesday of the month; Potts had gone to visit his sister. "He should return shortly," the hound reminded himself. He went back to his reading.

But Tilney did not return shortly. When the clock showed a quarter till seven, Barksdale set his book aside and went into the hall. He peered over the railing, but there was no sign of Potts at the door. "Some slight delay," the hound surmised. "Nothing of consequence, I'm certain." He returned to the drawing room.

Fifteen minutes later, Barksdale was back in the hall. He stayed there for several minutes, confident that if he simply kept looking for Potts, Potts would soon appear.

But Potts did not appear. "Well, a watched Potts never boils . . . or some such thing," said the hound. "No doubt he was having such a congenial visit with his family that he found it hard to leave. Nothing extraordinary in that. Nothing to be concerned about."

Barksdale went back to the drawing room and took up his

book once more. In spite of his own assurances, however, he was concerned. His eyes darted back and forth from the page to the clock.

You must concentrate, the hound scolded himself. *Mr. Dickens did not go to the trouble of bringing David Copperfield to life just so you could read his story with one eye on the clock! Potts will be here momentarily. Concentrate!*

But it was no use. The sufferings and strivings of David Copperfield, though related in the most vivid and entertaining manner, could not distract Barksdale from his present worries. He closed the book and placed it on the table.

The hound began to pace around the drawing room, making frequent detours to the hallway in the desperate hope that somehow Potts had returned without making the slightest noise. By eight-thirty he was pacing in the downstairs hall, stopping often to open the door and thrust his head outside. A light rain was falling—nothing unusual for London; nothing that would have kept Potts from home.

When the clock struck nine, Barksdale decided to take action. Throwing on his hat, coat, and gloves, the hound plunged into the evening gloom.

Nan Hodge bent toward the candle, straining her eyes to examine the row of stitches she had just sewn. Molly and Franny sat beside her at the table, working with their own needles. The other children were playing beneath the table. Fred sat on a wobbly stool beside the fire, smoking his pipe. Every now and then, he would feel himself tipping and thrust out a leg to steady himself.

"I needs to fix the legs on this stool," Fred declared. "It wobbles over-much."

"You has fixed them already, father," Franny reminded him.

"Which is probably why they wobbles so," murmured Molly.

"Well, then, I'm thinking the floor must be shifting," said Fred, bending over to study the planks.

"Ain't nothing wrong with the floor, Fred," Nan told him. "You just tend to the cheese shop and don't be getting no ideas about carpentry."

"I don't get ideas, Nan. As well you know."

"And we is all grateful for that, my dear," replied Nan, smiling at her husband.

Fred returned the smile and went back to smoking his pipe.

Liza stuck her head out from under the table. "Mummy," she said, "why did Uncle Tilney not come today? Doesn't he always come on this Wednesday? We miss him so."

"Do you miss your uncle or your uncle's sweets?" Nan teased.

Liza considered the question. "Well, they are both very nice," she replied.

"I am not certain why your uncle stayed away today," said Nan, with concern. "It's not like him to miss a visit. Surely if he had more pressing business, he would have sent word to us. I do hope he's not ill."

"Can't we go to Uncle Tilney's house and find out?" asked Liza.

"No, we cannot," answered Nan, who had been vexed by that thought many times already that evening. "We don't know where your uncle lives, you see? We don't know the address of his employer. We don't even know his employer's name," she added, looking away from her daughter's face.

"I don't know why he don't tell us," Fred declared. "It makes things difficult for a lot of people."

Something in Fred's voice caused Nan to lift her head from her needlework. She looked closely at her husband. "A lot of people?" she asked. "What do you mean by that, Fred Hodge?"

Fred quickly turned his face toward the fire. "I don't mean nothing, Nan. You know me, I never mean nothing."

"Fred Hodge," Nan repeated, in a commanding tone.

The rat turned sheepishly toward his wife.

"Fred Hodge, you has something on your mind," said Nan.

"Now, Nan, you know I never—"

"I don't want to hear that, Fred," Nan snapped. "I know you don't usually have anything on your mind. But I'm your wife, and I knows when you has something on your mind, and I knows it now."

Fred knew it was useless to deny Nan when Nan was in the right, which, in matters pertaining to himself, was nearly all the time. So Fred told his story. He told about the gentlemen of the committee, and the honor to Tilney, and how the gentlemen were planning to drop by at teatime that very day to inform Tilney of the honor. He didn't mention that the gentlemen had approved of his plans to carve a cheese bust of Her Majesty, figuring the less said about that the better.

"Only the gentlemen didn't drop by, as they said they would, so they must've had a previous engagement," Fred concluded. "Not that it mattered, what with Tilney not coming and all."

With deliberate slowness, Nan placed her sewing on the table in front of her. She gripped the edge of the table with the tips of her paws.

"Oh, Fred, what has you done?" she said, in a trembling voice.

Fred's mouth opened with surprise, so that his pipe fell into his lap and he had to brush the hot ashes off his pants. "Why, Nan—what do you mean? What is the matter?"

Nan's paws flew to her cheeks. "Those men, their questions, Tilney not coming today—it's too much of a coincidence, Fred. I've a bad feeling about it. Oh, why didn't you call me when they came into the shop?"

Fred's lips worked at his mustache. His eyebrows were hopping like crickets. "But, Nan, we don't know as something bad has happened to Tilney," he argued. "Anything could've kept him away today. And those committee blokes, they seemed square enough. They did, Nan. And all I told them was that Tilney was coming to tea. No more."

"Which was too much, Fred Hodge," Nan accused. "You is always saying too much or not enough and nothing in between."

Fred hung his head sorrowfully. "I suppose you is right,

Nan," he admitted. "But I sure didn't mean Tilney no harm."

"Mummy, did something bad happen to Uncle Tilney?" asked Liza, wide-eyed.

"No, child, no," Nan replied forcefully. "He'll be all right. I'm certain he will. I just wish I knew what to do. If only I knew where he lived."

"Wherever he lives," Molly said to Franny, "it's bound to be grander than here."

"Hush, girl!" Nan snapped at her daughter. "This is no time for your remarks. Your uncle may be in danger!"

The two girls blushed and cast their eyes to the floor. "Sorry, Mother," Molly murmured. "I weren't about wishing Uncle Tilney no harm."

Fred rose from his stool. "I'll go look for him," he said.

"Where will you look?" asked Nan.

"All over London, if I have to," said Fred. "If I lost him, then I ought to be the one to find him."

"Oh, Fred," Nan answered with a sigh, "you is a good soul. But it won't do no good for you to go running all over London in the dark and the rain by yourself."

"Then what are we to do, Nan?"

His wife shook her head. "I don't know," she said. "Maybe we should wait. Maybe there is nothing for us to worry about after all. Let's just wait and see."

Nan took up her sewing once again. Her daughters followed her lead. The younger children resumed their games under the table, though their voices were hushed now. Fred cleaned his pipe.

A short time later, there was a sharp knock on the door, which startled all of them and caused Fred to tumble off his stool.

Nan rushed to the door and threw it open.

The stranger was tall and well-dressed, his hat and coat glistening with rain. He raised his hat. "Mrs. Hodge?" he asked, in a deep voice.

Nan had never seen him before, but she knew who he must

be, even before he said, "I am Mr. Barksdale. Your brother Tilney is in my employ."

"Please come in, sir."

Having wiped his boots and removed his hat, Barksdale stepped into the room. He nodded to Fred and the children, who regarded him with a mixture of awe and curiosity. The hound, on the other hand, gazed at Nan and her family with such warmth and familiarity that they began to wonder if they had met him before.

"May I take your hat and coat, sir?" asked Nan.

"No, thank you," Barksdale replied. "I'm afraid my stay will be brief. Mrs. Hodge, has Tilney been to see you today?"

"No, sir. I'm sorry to say he has not."

"Were you expecting him?"

"We were, sir. He always comes to tea every other Wednesday. Has something happened to Tilney, sir?" Fear showed in Nan's eyes.

Barksdale frowned. "I don't know, Mrs. Hodge. All I can tell you is that your brother went out earlier today, he did not come here, and he has not returned home. And that is not at all like Potts."

"We may know a bit more than that, sir," said Nan. She proceeded to tell the hound about Fred's conversation with the pair of "committee men."

"A ferret and a one-eyed bear?" Barksdale asked Fred. "Are you certain?"

"Absolutely, sir," Fred replied. "I ain't never going to forget them two."

"Is that bad?" asked Nan.

"It isn't good," the hound told her. "But we need to know more. I must go." Barksdale donned his hat.

Nan placed her paw on his arm. "What can we do, sir?" she asked.

"There isn't much you can do right now," Barksdale replied. He smiled. "It may not be so bad. You mustn't worry." He paused, then added, "I don't think you should go to the police. Not yet."

"The police!" gasped Peter. "Crikey, is Uncle Tilney going to jail?"

"Don't be silly, Peter!" Nan scolded. "Your uncle ain't committed any crime. Ain't that right, Mr. Barksdale?" There was a trace of doubt in Nan's question.

"Your brother has done nothing wrong," Barksdale assured her. "Still, I think we ought not to involve the authorities at this time."

"Whatever you suggest, sir. But I will go to my father," she added. "He'll alert the family. We have relatives everywhere. Someone will have seen Tilney."

"Let me know if you hear anything," said Barksdale, reaching for the door.

"But how shall we contact you, sir?" asked Nan.

Barksdale halted with the door half open. At that moment, seeing the concern in Nan's eyes, the hound had the sudden urge to tell her the truth about everything. *Surely here is someone who will listen without judging,* he thought.

But he quickly abandoned the idea. It was dangerous to know too much about him; he had already put Tilney at risk—he had no desire to place others in peril. Besides, secrecy was a lifelong habit with him now; he could not give it up on a whim.

"You may contact me through Mr. Church, my solicitor," the hound replied. "He will know where to find me." Barksdale gave her the solicitor's address.

"Good luck to you, sir," said Nan. "Please, tell us if you find out anything."

"I promise to stay in touch, Mrs. Hodge."

Barksdale could tell from her eyes that she was disappointed—perhaps even insulted—by his lack of trust. But there was nothing he could do.

The hound departed, leaving the Hodges amazed and bewildered.

"So that's Tilney's employer," said Nan thoughtfully.

"He don't look like a maharaja," Peter declared.

"Still, he's a handsome gentleman," added Molly.

"He's not for you, girl," Nan quickly warned, causing Molly to blush.

"Who would be for her?" Daniel cracked.

Molly stuck out her tongue at her younger brother.

"Don't tease the girl," Fred scolded Daniel. "And, Molly, you won't get a beau making faces like that."

"I wish he'd brought his snake," said Peter. "That would be something to see."

"I should think not," Nan disagreed. "I'll have no snakes in this house. Snakes and little rats ain't a proper mix, for sure."

"But Uncle Tilney gets to—"

Nan cut him off. "Your Uncle Tilney is a grown rat and can do as he pleases," she said. "When you're grown up, you can live with a whole family of snakes, if you like."

"It'd be more exciting than this family," Molly grumbled.

"What's that you say?" her father asked.

"She weren't saying nothing," Franny answered for her older sister. "She were only humming a bit."

"She'd better start humming a different tune," warned Nan, glaring at her eldest daughter.

"I wish I'd never spoke to them 'committee men,'" said Fred, chomping on his pipe.

"We all wish that," Nan replied, shooting her husband a look of disapproval. "But wishes won't make a thing so, Fred. Wishes won't get my brother out of the pot you put him in."

To himself, Fred wished he had gone with Barksdale.

While the others were talking, Liza sat under the kitchen table, listening to the conversation and playing with her rag doll. Now she brought the doll close to her face. "I wish something, too," she whispered. "I wish that hound had brought sweets."

XIII

The Hound on the Roof

The steady rain had pushed pedestrians into London's cabs. Barksdale was nearly to the Strand before he was able to flag down an empty hansom.

"Brompton Road!" he shouted at the driver, before he folded himself into the seat.

"I should have known he would stoop to this," the hound fumed. "I should have known!" He beat his fist on his knee. "I should not have allowed Potts to go out alone. It was too dangerous."

When the cab reached Brompton Road, the hound allowed it to go several blocks past Renfield Place before ordering the driver to halt. Barksdale paid the fare and watched to make certain that the hansom drove away. Then he made his way back toward Renfield Place.

On this rainy night, the hound encountered few others on foot; still, he kept to the shadows. Thirty yards from the corner of Brompton Road and Renfield Place, he stopped. His nocturnal vision pierced the darkness ahead. He had expected the doctor to post a sentry at the corner—the ferret, possibly, or that bear—but Barksdale could detect no one lurking in the dark.

He proceeded to the corner. His gaze swept over the houses lining both sides of Renfield Place. Again, no one seemed to be about.

The hound knew the doctor's house, of course. But he did not intend to survey it from the pavement. Having first made certain that he was not observed, he went straight up the side of the house on the corner. As the hound climbed past the drawing room window, the gentleman within, combing his fingers through his thick whiskers as he sat by the fire, thought he saw a shadow sweep across the glass. But the gentleman's fire was so warm, his chair so comfortable, and his reveries so amusing, that he chose not to investigate. Which was just as well, for Barksdale was already up the wall and on the roof.

The houses in Renfield Place were all attached, so it was a simple matter for the hound to pass from rooftop to rooftop until he stood upon the cornice of the house directly across the street from Dr. Van Detta's residence. Barksdale squatted on his heels like a gargoyle, his stare fixed on the doctor's house. His coat was sodden with rain. Water dripped off his hat brim and trickled down his neck; but he did not notice.

From his perch on the rooftop, the hound scrutinized the doctor's house with his keen eyes. No one went in or out. No lights came on in the house. The drapes hung motionless in the windows.

After nearly an hour, Barksdale decided that he had seen all that could be seen from his roost. He stood up, stretched his legs, swung over the edge of the roof, and made his way silently to the ground. In a few swift strides, he crossed the street and leaped onto the face of Dr. Van Detta's house.

Climbing from window to window, Barksdale searched for a way in. On the second floor, he discovered a window standing open a few inches. The hound slid his paw into the crack. Slowly and quietly, he raised the sash, until he was able to slip inside.

It was an age when fashionable ladies and gentlemen crammed their boudoirs, libraries, and drawing rooms with great quantities of furniture and bric-a-brac that impeded movement and required daily dusting by the help. The room Barksdale had entered, however, contained only an iron bed and a high-backed wooden chair upon which some clothing had been hung. Plain as a monk's cell, it could only be a servant's room. That the room was occupied, Barksdale could tell from the steady breathing rising from the bed. Placing each step carefully on the floor, the hound moved silently toward the sleeper. He leaned over, peering at the figure beneath the bedclothes.

A pale face, and long brown hair falling over the pillow. *The doctor's maid*, Barksdale thought. As he watched, the woman murmured in her sleep and turned on her side. Her hair fell back from her cheek, exposing her jaw and her slender white throat.

Instantly, the hound's fur stood on end. He froze, holding his breath, while he stared down at the young woman's neck, which suddenly seemed to glow in the darkness. Barksdale could see the artery pulsing beneath the skin of her throat. Pum, pum, pum, pum—the beat of the rich red liquid flowing through the woman's veins.

Barksdale's own blood was pounding in his ears now. And each beat was like a command, urging him to do as his ancestors had done for centuries. Blood, blood, blood, blood. A sweet liqueur, the vampire's wine. He was not at fault. He was born with the curse. *If I am to die for being a vampire, why not live like one?* he reasoned.

Barksdale stepped closer to the bed. He bent over the maid. His lips parted.

Stop! his brain screamed. *You swore! You won't!*

Barksdale jerked upright. Covering his mouth with his paw, he backed away from the bed. His whole body was trembling. He shook his head violently until his mind seemed clear again. *Not tonight*, he vowed. *Not ever. If I am not stronger than my appetites, then I am lost.* Without looking back at the woman, the hound stepped lightly across the floor, eased the door open, and went out into the hall.

Room by room, floor by floor, Barksdale searched the quiet house. He located the master bedroom on the first floor. The bed had not been disturbed. In the drawing room, he shuffled through the papers on the doctor's desk. There was a cable from Paris informing Dr. Van Detta of a vampire sighting in Palermo. "London hunt completed?" the cable asked.

"No, it is not completed," Barksdale whispered harshly.

There was no sign of Potts on the first floor. The hound proceeded through the rooms on the ground floor, which were also empty. Finally, he crept downstairs to the basement. Someone was snoring loudly in a room off the kitchen. Barksdale slowly pushed the door open.

The butler was lying on his back, mouth agape, breath gurgling in his throat like water rushing down a drainpipe. The hound approached cautiously. A table beside the bed held a candle and a box of matches. Barksdale struck a match and lit the candle. The wick flared, illuminating a corner of the room and the butler's narrow bed.

The butler's snoring halted abruptly. He closed his mouth, smacking his thin lips several times. His face wore a pained expression, as he pinched his eyelids to shut out the light. Finally, a sliver of eyeball appeared beneath his left lid. The drowsy eye slowly focused on the dark figure standing beside the bed. The eyelid closed again. Seconds later, both eyes shot open. The butler cried out in fear and pulled the bedclothes over his head.

"Take what you want," said a quavering voice from beneath the covers. "The keys to the silver are on the bureau. Please, don't hurt me."

"I am not here to rob," answered Barksdale. "Where is Dr. Van Detta?"

The bedclothes stopped shaking.

"He's in his bed," said the butler.

"He is not in his bed," the hound replied. "Where is he? I want to know now."

The butler's bony fingers appeared at the edge of the bedclothes. Slowly he inched the coverlet down, until his face was visible. He looked the intruder over from head to foot.

"Where is the doctor?" Barksdale demanded again.

"He's not in his bed?"

"I told you that already," said the hound, growling impatiently.

"If he's not in his bed, then I'm sure I don't know where he is," the butler declared.

"When did you last see him?"

"He went out early this afternoon. With his two associates." The butler made a face to show his distaste for Slatkin and Chuggers.

"Where did they go?"

"I have no idea, sir."

"Did he say when they would return?"

"He didn't tell me anything, sir."

The hound grabbed the butler by the front of his nightshirt. "Are you telling me the truth?" he growled, showing his teeth.

The butler cringed, stretching his face away from the threatening fangs. "I don't know anything, sir. I swear it!"

Barksdale let the man fall back on the bed. "All right," he said. "When you see your master again, tell him this: If he harms my servant in any way, then he will suffer a terrible punishment. Tell him that, do you hear?"

The butler nodded rapidly.

The hound made his way back upstairs and left by the front door. He saw no point in remaining in the neighborhood; whatever Dr. Van Detta was planning, he apparently was not going to bring Tilney Potts to Renfield Place.

Barksdale caught another cab, which he ordered to drive back and forth along the route Potts would normally have taken on his way to his sister's home. Once, the hound leaped from the cab, thinking he had spotted his servant coming out of a coffeehouse. But it was only a mole, headed for his shift at a jam factory across the river. Finally, with the day coming on, Barksdale got out of the cab at Ludgate Hill. Though it was still raining, he had decided to walk home. It would make him more wet and miserable; he felt that was the least he deserved.

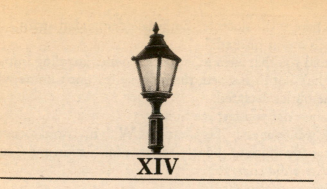

XIV

Master and Father

As Barksdale drew near Harker Lane, his hopes began to revive. Perhaps Potts would be waiting for him at home, ready to tell how he had fallen asleep on a bus, been locked inside a museum, or decided to visit a friend in the country. *There are plenty of reasons for Potts to be absent,* Barksdale assured himself. *I will hope for the best and take the worst as it comes.*

His spirits lifted, the hound walked faster and faster, so that he was nearly running by the time he reached home. He burst through the door, shouting, "Potts! Tilney Potts! Are you here?"

Barksdale stood motionless in the hall. With his sharp ears, he could hear every clock ticking, every pipe dripping, every floorboard cracking—but no reply from Potts.

The hound shut the door and trudged upstairs to the bedroom, where he pulled off his muddy boots and removed his wet clothing. He stood in the middle of the room, wondering what to do with his dirty clothes. What did Potts do with the laundry? Every week there were clean shirts and collars, pressed suits, and polished boots in his closet. That was Potts's doing. How did he do it? Every day Potts brought him his meals. Where did the food come from? How did they get coal? Potts arranged it. Potts arranged everything. How could he ever get along without Potts?

Barksdale put on his dressing gown. He took the dirty clothes downstairs to the kitchen, where he left them in a pile on the table. He realized that he hadn't eaten anything since lunch the previous day. The cast-iron stove was cold, of course; Potts made up the fire every morning. Barksdale could have fired the stove himself, but he decided that he had neither time nor energy to spare. He found some bread in the breadbox and some butter in the icebox. He sliced the bread, buttered it, and ate it leaning against the stove. There was milk in the icebox to wash it down. He did not object to such simple fare. He still remembered how it felt to be grateful for bread and butter.

The hound went back upstairs. He looked at himself in the mirror above his dresser. The fur on his neck was damp and matted. His eyes were dull and cloudy. He ought to lie down, but there was no time for that. Perhaps if he took a bath . . . but there was no time for that, either. Potts was still missing.

Barksdale moved to the washstand, intending to scrub his face, at least. The basin was empty. Potts was not there to fill it.

Barksdale sighed, slumping over the washstand. "This is too inconvenient, Mr. Potts," he moaned. "It's not right for you to disappear." Then the hound did something he had not done since he was a pup. He threw back his head and howled—a long, mournful, despondent wail. The cry arched above Oxford Street, causing the druggist nearby to spill a stomach powder and the horses of a passing coach to stamp and rear.

Barksdale immediately felt embarrassed by the outburst. It made him think back to a time when he was young. He and his mother were in the kitchen of their two-room flat in Camden Town; the "little place," as they called it later—the house before the inheritance. The hound had accidentally stepped on his favorite toy, a wooden cavalryman riding a wheeled horse. A wheel had cracked off. Sad and angry, he had howled like wind in the chimney.

His mother put down her sewing and picked up the broken

pieces. "It's not so bad as all that," she said. "You will only need some glue."

Barksdale continued to wail; but then, it is doubly painful to know that you are both unhappy and the cause of your own unhappiness.

"You may howl if you like," his mother said patiently, "but it seems a waste. You must either learn to live with what is broken, or you must fix it."

She spoke from experience, Barksdale knew, for she had lived many years with a broken heart. Her husband, Barksdale's father, had gone away when Barksdale was three years old. The elder Barksdale had taken ship for America, where he had plunged into the maelstrom of the American Civil War and vanished forever. The hound had always assumed that vampirism was at the heart of his father's disappearance, but his mother never explained, and he, wishing to spare his mother's feelings, never asked for an explanation. Barksdale's mother never got over the loss; of that he was certain. It etched two lines across her forehead and blunted the edges of her smile.

His mother's eyes were blue-gray, like his own. The hound kept a small hand-tinted picture of her in an oval frame on his dressing table. He took it from the table now, cradling it gently in his paw. In the picture, his mother—so young, so beautiful, so happy—wore a dress with blue and white stripes and a white lace collar. At her throat was the ivory cameo Barksdale's father had given her before they were married. She had often worn that cameo—a souvenir of happier times—even after her husband had disappeared.

Barksdale returned the picture carefully to the dresser.

His mother was the only family he had ever known—unless he included Potts.

He *did* include Potts.

Barksdale brushed his fur briskly, donned clean clothes, and went out.

* * *

Nan Hodge had also spent a sleepless night. When morning finally came, she had fed her children breakfast and shooed them outside. She had washed and dried and stacked the dishes. She had swept the floor and polished the table. She had mended her children's clothing and finished her sewing. She had washed the dirty clothes and hung them to dry on the line in the alley. Then she had scrubbed the stoop. She had done all this while tiptoeing around her father, Ephraim Potts, who sat stonily at her kitchen table, his eyes fixed on the window, as if he expected a bird to light on the sill and bring him news.

Nan stood in the middle of the kitchen, rubbing her paws on her apron, looking around for some task that remained to be done. The window could be washed, she supposed. Or she could air the bedding.

As he had done off and on all morning, Fred stuck his head into the room, his eyebrows raised as if to ask, "Any news?" Nan shook her head. Fred frowned and ducked back into the shop.

"He needn't stay out of my way," Ephraim Potts rumbled. "I don't blame him."

"I don't blame him either," said Nan. "At least, not so much anymore. But that doesn't matter. He blames himself."

"Fred's a good fellow," said her father, nodding as he spoke, so that his silvery whiskers folded against his chest. "He works hard. He does right by you and your kids, Nan."

"I know it, Father."

"I won't say he don't get peculiar notions now and again. But that ain't such a terrible fault. And he has you to rein him in."

"Would you like some tea, Father?" Nan asked.

"Fred's a son a father could be proud of. There's nothing dishonorable about Fred."

"I won't argue with you there, Father," said Nan. "And then, you have your own sons to be proud of."

"And daughters," Ephraim added, looking at Nan. "I always been proud of my children, most of 'em. You don't have to be rich," he said. "You don't have to be knighted by the Queen. You don't even have to live your life the way your mum and I dreamed it for you, rocking you in our arms when you was a baby. But you don't have to shame your mother and father, neither."

"And we don't none of us do it, Father," Nan replied. "Not a one. Nor Tilney neither."

"He done it already," her father said. "And now he's gone from bad to worse."

"We don't know that," Nan objected.

"I don't see how it can turn out else," her father argued. "He's turned his back on his family. How can it turn out else?"

Nan was already upset. She did not wish to twist her emotions further by quarreling with her father. She decided to wash the window.

The day rolled slowly across London. Old Mr. Potts sat at the table, watching the light come and go from the window, while Nan fidgeted. She sat down and stood up, opened the door and shut it. Fearing for her brother, she spoke sharply to her husband and children. She did again all the cleaning she had done during the morning.

In the late afternoon, Peter rushed in from outside. "Mother, the gentleman is back!" he said breathlessly. "Uncle Tilney's employer."

Ephraim Potts snapped his head toward the door, a fierce light glowing in his eyes. Nan hurried to the doorway and looked out.

Mr. Barksdale was splashing down the alley, the Hodge children trailing him like a brood of ducklings. As he caught sight of Nan, the hound removed his hat.

"Mrs. Hodge, have you any word of your brother?"

"I'm afraid not," said Nan. "My uncles and cousins are searching for him, but so far, he has not been found."

Barksdale frowned. "I searched for him also, all last night and today, with the same result."

"You look tired, sir," said Nan. "Won't you come in and

120

have some tea? It's real tea, sir," she added quickly, "from India."

"Thank you, Mrs. Hodge," said Barksdale. "I would be most grateful for a cup."

Nan led the hound inside, where she introduced him to her father.

"I am honored to meet you, Mr. Potts," said Barksdale, bowing to the old rat. Good manners stipulated that Barksdale, being younger than Mr. Potts, could not offer his paw unless the old gentleman offered his paw first; Mr. Potts, however, kept his arm at his side. He said nothing, but looked the hound up and down with a severe gaze.

"Do be seated, please, sir," said Nan. "I'll put on the kettle." She gave her father a glance that was both a plea and a warning, but the old rat refused to meet her eyes. He stared boldly at the hound, who slid wearily into a seat opposite him.

"Where is my son?" Ephraim Potts demanded.

"Father!" said Nan.

"It is all right, Mrs. Hodge," said Barksdale. "It is the question which is uppermost in my own mind, I assure you." He stroked his muzzle thoughtfully. "I don't know the whereabouts of your son, Mr. Potts. I have searched everywhere. I fear . . . " He hesitated. He looked at Nan, who had frozen in the act of placing the kettle on the grate. "I fear Tilney has been kidnapped."

Nan stifled a cry with her paw. "Kidnapped?" said Ephraim Potts. "Why would anyone want to kidnap my son?"

Barksdale frowned. "It is likely on account of his association with myself."

"What did I tell ya?" Ephraim Potts exclaimed, turning to his daughter. He pointed to the hound. "I told ya all along this gentleman were not a proper gentleman. Now ya see how it has turned out! Tilney kidnapped!"

"Father, I don't think you're being just to Mr. Barksdale," Nan countered.

"It's justice he needs, all right," her father declared. "The justice of Newgate Prison and the Lord High Executioner. That's the justice for his kind!"

"I swear to you, Mr. Potts," said the hound, "I am not a criminal."

"Then why do you hide?" the rat argued. "Why is my son ashamed to name your name or tell where you live? Honest men are not afraid to show their faces."

"Stop it, Father!" cried Nan, leaning over the table. "Mr. Barksdale is not hiding now, is he? He is here to help Tilney. He is a good and kind gentleman. It was him sent the doctor when my Liza had the croup." A look of surprise passed briefly over Barksdale's face. "He's not what you think he is."

Barksdale felt a twinge of fear. Had Potts already told his sister everything?

"Then why has he got Tilney kidnapped? What's he mixed up in?" asked Ephraim Potts.

"Again, I swear to you," Barksdale said, "my only crime is that I was born." He turned to Nan for help.

"Father," she said, taking the old rat's paw, "I believe we must trust in Mr. Barksdale, as Tilney does. Tilney would never think so highly of him, if it were not deserved."

Ephraim Potts stared into his daughter's eyes for a moment. Then he turned to the hound. The anger eased from his face, but he remained wary.

"I still want to know why my son has been kidnapped," he said.

Barksdale removed his gloves and slipped them into his pocket. "I believe I can shed some light on the matter. For the past several months, I have been evading a man who wishes to harm me," the hound explained. "Since he was unable to track me down, he has adopted a new strategy; I fear he has kidnapped your son in order to draw me out."

"Why is he after you?"

"It is a personal matter," said Barksdale. "He has a grudge against me, though I have never done him any wrong."

"Why don't you go to the police?" asked Mr. Potts.

The hound brushed an invisible crumb from the table. "Perhaps I should have," he said ruefully. "At the time, I thought I was protecting myself by not going to the police."

"We should go to them now," Ephraim Potts urged.

"No," the hound replied. "My enemy is a vengeful man. If he thinks we have set the Yard on him, he may harm your son."

"Then what are we to do?" asked Nan. "I mean, we don't know where Tilney is. We don't even know for certain that he has been kidnapped. Shouldn't the kidnappers be asking for a ransom?"

Barksdale nodded. "That's what puzzles me," he said. "If Tilney has been kidnapped, why haven't we been contacted?"

The kettle was boiling. Nan dropped the tea leaves into the teapot—one scoop each for Mr. Barksdale, her father, and herself, plus "one for the pot." She poured the water over the leaves. While she waited for the tea to brew, Nan fetched the crockery from the cupboard. With chagrin, she noted the stains and chips on the cups and saucers. How could she serve a gentleman's tea in such common dishes?

Then Nan remembered. Excusing herself, she went into the bedroom. There was a wooden trunk beside her bed. She knelt and opened the lid. In the bottom of the trunk was a biscuit tin. Inside the tin was a parcel carefully wrapped in a red cotton cloth. Nan slowly removed the cloth, revealing a cup and saucer of white porcelain. She took these back to the kitchen.

When Nan served the tea minutes later, Barksdale immediately noted that his cup and saucer were much finer than the crockery being used by Nan and her father. One side of his cup was decorated with a painting of the Crystal Palace; the other side bore the legend "1851." A garland of painted roses ringed the saucer.

"Mrs. Hodge, you have gone to too much trouble for me," said the hound. "I don't deserve to drink from a family heirloom."

"You are a most deserving guest," Nan replied. "And it were no trouble."

Ephraim Potts squinted at the cup. "That were your mum's, weren't it?" he asked his daughter.

"It were," said Nan. "She won it at the Great Exhibition," she explained to Barksdale. "You know, in 1851, as it says there."

In 1851, more than six million people had come from all over the globe to visit the Great Exhibition in Hyde Park. They came to gawk at the industrial marvels of the day, all of them enclosed in a structure that was itself marvelous: a nineteen-acre exhibition hall of prefabricated steel and glass dubbed "The Crystal Palace."

"We was newlyweds, my Dora and me," Ephraim Potts recounted, "and poor as church rats. But somehow we scraped together the bus fare across London to Hyde Park, plus two shillings for the admission. I never seen such things as they showed there. The steam hammer and the sewing machine, the mechanical reaper and the telegraph. Oh, you is used to them now; they're common as bedbugs. But back then, they was like miracles. They even had a garden bench carved entirely from coal. Can you believe it? I unloaded tons of coal in my day, but I don't think none of it ever got made into furniture. Though many's the cold night I wished I could turn furniture into coal!"

Barksdale and Nan smiled into their teacups.

"But them is memories of happy times long ago," said the old rat, stroking his beard. "Times when I had good work and my Dora was still alive. Times which is no help in our present troubles. So I'm asking you now, sir: how are we to find my son?"

The hound set down his teacup. He rubbed his tired eyes with his paw. "I wish I could tell you, Mr. Potts. I'm certain that we will be contacted. We must wait and hope."

"And keep searching," said Ephraim Potts. "Hope ain't nothing compared to a rat's nose sniffing in every corner of this city."

"Yes, we must keep searching. You're right, of course," said

Barksdale. He stood up from the table. "Mrs. Hodge, thank you most kindly for the tea. I shall continue my own search and check back with you later. I beg you, if you should hear anything from the kidnappers, please consult with me before you take any action."

"We will do as you ask, Mr. Barksdale," Nan replied. She looked to her father, but the old rat stared deliberately out of the window.

The hound was moving toward the door when Fred burst in from the shop, accompanied by a chubby rat wearing pince-nez glasses.

"Nan! Nan! News, Nan! He found it! Cousin Simon found it!" cried Fred.

"Found what, Fred?" Nan asked, with annoyance. "Can't you see Mr. Barksdale is here?"

"Oh," said Fred, stopping short. "Pleased to see you, Mr. Barksdale."

"And I to see you, Mr. Hodge. What have you found?"

"A notice about Tilney," Fred replied, slapping a newspaper down on the table. "Here, in *The Times*."

"*The Times!* Of course!" said Barksdale, thumping his hat against his leg. "I should have thought of it!"

"I read *The Times* every morning," Cousin Simon stated. "It pays to keep up, don't you think? At least, I think it does, especially for a rat in my profession. I mean, when you write advertising copy, you have to know what people are talking about. At least, I think you do."

"And he found this notice right here," Fred broke in. He pointed to the words in bold type.

T. Potts to trade. Bramstoke Wharf. 10 P.M. Come alone.

"It's a curious message, really," Cousin Simon observed. "Rather cryptic. I do, however, commend the writer for his brevity. Brevity is the soul of copywriting. You can't be too plain or too brief. Or rather, you can be plain and brief. At least, I think you can."

"The notice says, 'to trade,'" Nan remarked. "Trade for what? They don't mention money."

"I don't think they want money," Barksdale replied.

The rats looked at each other uncertainly, as if they already guessed the answer to their next question but were not sure how best to put it.

Finally, Nan said, "They want you, Mr. Barksdale? But then . . . what shall we do? We can't just let . . . I mean, if it were money . . . "

"You needn't worry, Mrs. Hodge," the hound assured her. "Your brother and I will both come out all right."

"Bramstoke Wharf," said Fred. "It's not far."

Ephraim Potts grasped Fred by the arm. "You go now and collect all the uncles and cousins you can find. Tell them to meet me at the wharf at sunset. And Fred—tell them there may be trouble. They should bring whatever's to hand for bashing a man on the head. Go!"

Fred started toward the door.

"Mr. Hodge, wait!" Barksdale commanded.

Fred halted, looking hesitantly from Nan's father to the hound.

Barksdale addressed old Mr. Potts. "You mustn't send an army to rescue Tilney, sir. It would be a grave mistake."

"And why not?" Ephraim Potts replied. "Do you expect us to wait around here for the fairies to bring him home?"

"The kidnappers will be watching," argued the hound. "They'll see you coming."

"Rats do very well at not being seen, sir."

"I don't doubt it," Barksdale responded, "but you cannot hide an army. If they see you coming, they may spirit Tilney away, or worse."

"Then I'll go myself," Ephraim Potts decided.

"Father, you can't," said Nan.

"Why not, daughter?"

"You're too . . . Father, you're not well enough."

"Tilney is my son!" the old rat roared, banging his fist on the table. "Who better to help him?"

"I'll do it," said Barksdale. "I'm the one they want. If I go, no one will get hurt."

"That's very brave of you, sir," Nan answered. "But what will you say to these people? Are you sure they'll let Tilney go?"

"I believe they will. Tilney can do them no harm, so they have no need to harm him."

"Or you, sir?" asked Nan.

The hound smiled reassuringly. "I shall live to see Liza's grandchildren," he said. Nan tried to return a confident grin, but the worry would not lift from her face.

"Do you even know Bramstoke Wharf?" Ephraim Potts asked the hound.

"I can find it."

"It's no place for a gentleman to be roaming around in the dark."

"Like you, Mr. Potts, I do very well in the dark."

"No," the old rat insisted, "someone should go with you."

"I'll go," Fred volunteered.

"Fred Hodge, you will not!" his wife countered.

"I will, Nan," replied Fred, his jaw set. "I got Tilney into this mess and I'll help get him out. I will, Nan, and even you won't never put me off it, no matter how long or how loud you talks at me!"

Nan's face grew red. She sputtered at her husband, as if she were about to launch a tirade, but all her arguments seemed to slip from her lips. Flabbergasted, she turned to the hound. "But the message said you was to come alone. Ain't that right, Mr. Barksdale?"

"The notice was quite specific on that point," Cousin Simon put in. "At least, it seemed specific to me."

"That is true," said the hound. "And I am reluctant to do anything that would endanger Tilney or anyone else."

Nan sighed with relief.

"But," Barksdale went on, "Tilney may require assistance after his release. Fred, if you are agreed, I will gladly accept your offer."

"At your service, Mr. Barksdale," Fred replied.

"Very well. I have other matters to attend to now. But I shall return at exactly nine this evening. In the meantime," he looked at old Mr. Potts, "please promise me that you will not attempt to rescue Tilney on your own."

The old rat stared coolly at the hound. "We will promise." He pointed a crooked finger at Barksdale. "But I also want a promise from you."

"What is that?" asked the hound.

"Promise me that once Tilney has returned, you will release him from your service."

"Father!" Nan gasped.

Barksdale did not hesitate. "You have my word," he said. Bowing to the rats, he opened the door and went out.

"Father, you needn't have done that," Nan complained. "I'm certain that Tilney would not wish it."

"I know what's best for Tilney," her father snapped. "And so does that hound. He agreed readily enough, didn't he? Now, Fred, you keep your eye on that Barksdale as you would a snake. He ain't to be trusted."

"He's an honorable gentleman," Fred replied. "I feel strongly that he is."

"Like I said—you don't let him out of your sight."

"And don't you be getting heroic, Fred Hodge," Nan ordered, though her chin was trembling.

"Now, Nan," said Fred, "you know I don't never get heroic." He wrapped his arm firmly about his wife's waist. Fred's legs, however, were wobbling.

XV

Prisoner Potts

Twenty-four hours earlier, Tilney Potts ambled along Newgate Street. The pavement, still wet from the morning rain, glistened in the afternoon sun. Swinging his arms as he walked, the little rat hummed a tune, happy to be out on such a fine day, happy that his right shoulder was finally free of pain. He had a pocket full of sweets for his nieces and nephews and the prospect of a pleasant visit with his sister.

A barrel-chested stranger burst out of the throng of pedestrians ahead of Tilney. The man, whose expression indicated that he was on a mission of the utmost importance, hastened toward the rat. Tilney veered to one side to allow the man to pass, but to his surprise, instead of rushing by him, the stranger stopped directly in his path.

"Mr. Potts?" said the stranger urgently. "You are Mr. Tilney Potts, are you not?"

"Yes," Tilney replied. "I am. I don't believe—"

"A terrible accident, Mr. Potts," the man uttered, his face and voice full of woe. "It's your sister—Mrs. Hodge. Simply terrible. You must come at once."

"What?" said Tilney, both confused and alarmed. "An accident? What accident? Has something happened to Nan?"

The stranger gripped Tilney's arm, drawing him along as they spoke. "It grieves me to tell it, Mr. Potts. She was on her way to Petticoat Square. Going to pick out some clothes for the children, no doubt. A wonderful mother, your sister. And then a man dropped a bottle of ginger beer. It broke like a shot, which spooked a carriage horse. The horse bolted. Your sister was just crossing the street. She couldn't get out of the way."

"Was she hurt?" asked Tilney.

"I'm afraid so," said the stranger, shaking his head sorrowfully.

"How badly?" Tilney demanded. He was walking as fast as his short legs would carry him, with the stranger's arm guiding him along the streets.

"God only knows, sir. They sent for a doctor."

Tilney did not know what to imagine, but he could not help imagining the worst. Nan's body lay bruised and bleeding. She was calling for him. She was gasping for breath. Her voice was a whisper. *Nan! Hold on, Nan!*

"Where is she now?" asked Tilney.

"A room off Bishopsgate, sir. They were trying to make her comfortable. It's not far."

"Does her husband know?"

"Someone went to fetch him. He should be there before us. I was sent to look for you. Mrs. Hodge most especially asked to see you."

"Pray God we're not too late," said Tilney, a lump forming in his throat. "It was lucky you were able to find me. How did you recognize me?"

"I've glimpsed you at the cheese shop many a time," the man replied. "I live just across the street, you see."

"I'm grateful to you, sir," said Tilney, "though I'm afraid I don't know your name."

"It's just here, Mr. Potts." The stranger pointed a meaty finger at an alley up ahead. He tightened his grip on Tilney's arm.

"I thought you said she was near Bishopsgate?" Tilney questioned.

"Did I?" asked the stranger. "I must have been mistaken." He steered the rat into the alley. A door opened. The stranger pushed Tilney through the door.

It took a moment for Tilney's eyes to adjust to the gloom. Then, in the dim light seeping through the dirty window, he saw the ferret and the bear. Oddly enough, his first thought was, *Why would those two be looking after my sister?* And then he realized what was happening; but it was already too late.

Tilney Potts sat on the dusty floor of the flat, his back against the crumbling plaster. Coils of rope bound his arms to his sides. A handkerchief had been wedged between his teeth and tied behind his head, forcing him to wear a desperate smile.

The man who had accosted him—Tilney now knew this must be Dr. Van Detta—had gone out with the bear, leaving Tilney alone with the ferret. Since the departure of the others, the ferret had been pacing the length of the small room, muttering and wringing his paws. From time to time, he had plunked himself down on a packing crate—the only piece of "furniture" in the room—but almost immediately he had jumped up and resumed pacing.

"Kidnapping!" the ferret groaned, as he prowled back and forth like a leopard in a cage. "Kidnapping! In all my days, with all my crimes, I ain't never done nothing like this. I don't like it. I do not like it, I tell you!" He tore the hat from his head and dashed it on the floor. "It is all the fault of that doctor. I knowed he were no good. I knowed it! I shoulda never thrown in with him. Now look what he has got me into. Kidnapping! In all my days, kidnapping!"

"Leez—sir," said Tilney, through the gag.

The ferret halted and looked at the rat. "You say something?"

"Leez—sir. Tay—croff agag."

"I can't understand you with that thing in your mouth."

Tilney nodded vigorously.

"Oh," said the ferret, "you wants me to remove the gag?"

Tilney nodded again.

The ferret looked around. "I ain't certain the doctor would approve of that."

Tilney's eyes were pleading.

The ferret shrugged. "Oh, well, who says I gots to do everything that doctor tells me, hey? If I'd thought for myself, I wouldn't be here right now." He started to bend toward the rat, then stepped back. He pointed a finger at Tilney's nose. "If I takes it off, will you promise not to call for help?"

Tilney nodded in agreement.

The ferret stooped and unbound the gag. With his face unfettered once again, Tilney worked his jaw and licked his lips. "Thank you," he said.

"No bother," the ferret replied. He walked across the room and sank to the floor, slumping against the wall opposite Tilney.

"My sister is all right, then?" Tilney asked earnestly.

The ferret cocked his head to one side. "Your sister?" he said. "How should I know about your sister? I don't know nothing about my own sisters. Why should I know about yours?"

"That man." Tilney looked toward the door. "The one who brought me here—he said my sister had been injured in an accident. But I believe it was a trick."

"Oh, that." The ferret shrugged. "He were just having you on. Your sister ain't been in no accident that I know of. Not that accidents ain't happening all the time in this city. Why, just last week, I fell out a window when the landlord come to collect the rent."

"I'm relieved to know my sister is safe," said Tilney.

"'Course she's safe," the ferret replied. "You is the one what's in trouble. You and me, that is. Don't know how either one of us will find our way out this mess." The ferret pulled threads from the end of his coat.

"There's a very simple solution to your problem, Mr. Slatkin," Tilney observed.

"How you know my name?" asked the ferret suspiciously.

"I heard the bear call you that."

The ferret slapped the floor with his paw. "See there? See what I is up against? How can a bloke get anywhere when he is up against that kind of ignorance? I told Chuggers he was never to call me by name in front of you. It ain't safe, you see. Suppose you was to go to the police about this kidnapping. You might, you know. It's the kind of thing I'd go to the police about, except for the fact that the police would likely clap me in irons right off and leave me to rot. But if I was you, and I went to the police, well, then I could tell them to look, not just for any ferret, but for a ferret what is known as Slatkin, alias me. Which makes it a lot easier to find me, which that bear-brained Chuggers don't never even think about!"

"I sympathize with your predicament," said Tilney. "It must be terribly trying to work with such incompetents."

"That's what it is, all right," Slatkin replied. "It's nin— competence. That's what it is."

"But I do believe there's a simple solution."

The ferret pulled at his right ear. He gave the rat a long look. "Such as?"

"You could let me go."

The ferret laughed. "And have you run straight to Scotland Yard? Not likely, mate."

"But I wouldn't go to Scotland Yard or any other authority," said Tilney. "My master, you see—he is a very private gentleman."

"On account of him being a vampire."

"Yes. That's the main reason. So I couldn't go to the police."

Slatkin thought that over for a minute. "So the police don't get involved. So maybe your master, he handles the matter on his own," said the ferret. "Maybe some night old Slatkin wakes up with Mr. Barksdale's fangs in his throat. What about that?"

"But he would never do that," Tilney insisted. "Mr. Barksdal has sworn never to make use of the vampire bite. You may tru him to stay true to his word."

The ferret scratched his head. "Yeah, well, I got my own wor to be true to, don't I? And I told this doctor I would help hir find your Mr. Barksdale, which I ain't done yet, though would've done it, mind, if the doctor had been a bit mor patient. We was on the trail, Chuggers and me. We was close I'd've had that hound already, if it hadn't been for Chuggers larking about like he does."

"Still," said Tilney, shaking his head. "Kidnapping. That is serious offense."

"Don't you think I know it?" wailed the ferret, beating hi breast. "It is now like a millstone around my scrawny neck. Me who ain't never kidnapped as much as a fly in my whole rotter life. It ain't fair, I tell you."

"Let me go," Tilney urged. "Free me, and you free yourself."

Slatkin sat up. He rocked his head from side to side. "Th doctor ain't a man to be crossed," he stated.

"You're not afraid of him, surely?"

"I ain't?" said the ferret. "And why shouldn't I be? You thin he wouldn't snap my neck in a second if he thought I'd crosse him? You know he would. 'Course, if I had that bear to back m up . . . but he ain't the most reliable bear you ever seen, unles you is relying on him to be unreliable."

"You could do it," Tilney argued, "with or without the bear."

The ferret coughed. "Well, I don't know. The matter ain't s simple as it seems." He gave Tilney a look of helplessness. "It' about money, too, you see. If I don't get money from the doctor then I can't pay what I owes to Toby Thigpen. And if I don't pa Toby, yours truly is going to wind up in a pot of glue."

"I'll see that you get the money," Tilney promised.

"Really?" Slatkin was growing more interested.

"Whatever you need."

"Now that is an offer worth considering," said the ferret, stroking his chin. He leaped up from the floor and resumed pacing.

"But you must decide quickly, Mr. Slatkin, before your friends return."

"Oh, they ain't no friends of mine," Slatkin stated. "Well, maybe that Chuggers, in a way, though I don't know why I ever made him my partner. But that doctor, now—"

"Mr. Slatkin, we haven't much time."

"Not much time. Then . . . well . . . let's see—you promise about the money?"

"You have my word."

The ferret took another turn around the room. Then he stopped, placed his hands on his hips, and nodded resolutely.

"All right, Mr. Rat," he said. "We has a de—"

At that moment, the door flew open. Dr. Van Detta stepped into the room, slamming the door behind him. He bore a large canvas bag, which he slipped from his shoulder and dropped on the floor with a thud.

"Is our visitor comfortable?" he asked, smiling at Tilney. His smile faded to a look of disapproval. He turned on Slatkin.

"Who told you to remove the gag?" he barked.

"Nobody," Slatkin replied, shrinking against the wall. "I just thought I might question him, you know? Maybe get some information. He gave me his word he wouldn't raise a ruckus."

"Did he?" said the doctor. "And did he also give you the information you were seeking?"

"I reckon not. You come back before I could really grill him."

"It's good that I did," Van Detta said. "Imagine how stunned I would be if you had actually discovered anything useful. Now get in the alley with the bear and keep an eye out for that hound."

Slatkin and Tilney exchanged sympathetic glances. The ferret put on his hat. "Ain't nobody going nowhere," he murmured, as he slipped out the door.

Having swiped at the dusty crate with his handkerchief, Dr. Van Detta seated himself upon it, giving Tilney a view of his broken profile. The doctor removed his hat. Leaning forward, elbows resting on his thighs, he tapped the hat idly against the inside of his calf, while his gaze penetrated the floor in front of him.

Tilney had already concluded that the rest of the building was vacant. He heard no babies wailing, no children shouting, no boots booming on the wooden floors, no pipes rattling. The only sounds came from the street, which was so noisy that, even if he had cried out, no one would have heard him above the din of traffic.

"I hope my little story about your sister did not cause you undue anxiety," the doctor said.

Tilney knew he ought to be afraid of this man, but all he could feel was anger. "It was cruel," he snapped, glaring at Van Detta.

"A necessary deception, I'm afraid," the doctor responded. "I assure you, I mean you and your family no harm."

"Then why am I a prisoner?"

"Can't you guess?"

"You think Mr. Barksdale will try to rescue me."

"I know Mr. Barksdale will try to rescue you."

"What if he doesn't?" Tilney suggested.

"But he will, Mr. Potts. Just to make certain, I have told him where he may find you tonight. He will not abandon you, you may be sure. He has too much pride, for one thing. And you know what the Bible says about pride."

"Why must you harm him?" Tilney challenged. "He has never harmed you. He has never harmed anyone."

Dr. Van Detta turned to face Tilney. "Your master is a monster, Mr. Potts. He is a vampire. Do you know what a single vampire can do to a village? Allow me to describe it to you. First, the monster selects an innocent victim—a young woman or a child . . . or even a rat, perhaps. The monster does not care whom it infects. No, the monster cares only for its own despicable desires. It wants only what it wants." The doctor leaned toward Tilney, his blue eyes locked on the face of the rat. "So the vampire waits . . . and it watches—and then, in the black of night, the vampire strikes!" Doctor Van Detta's right hand shot out, clawing the air.

Tilney jumped, cracking his head against the wall behind him. "Ow!" he cried.

"Are you all right?" asked the doctor.

Tilney blinked several times. The back of his head hurt. He wished he were free to rub it. "You startled me," he muttered.

"That was my intent," said Dr. Van Detta. He continued his story.

"The vampire seizes his prey. He fastens his jaws to the victim's throat. He drinks greedily. And as he drinks, he infects his victim with the vampire curse. Believe me, it is a plague equal to the Black Death. In a matter of days, these victims are pale and shuddering, wracked by the unholy desires of the monster who attacked them. The weak ones will die outright. But the stronger ones—a few days more and they seem to recover, except that their skin has a bluish tint. This is merely a sign, however, that the curse has entered a second—more ghastly—phase. By the next full moon, the vampire's victims are hunting their own prey. Friend stalks friend. Mothers infect their own children. Soon the entire village is mad with fear. There is a frenzy of accusation. Innocent people, you may be sure, are condemned along with guilty vampires. Meanwhile, the monsters that have escaped detection are free to seek out more victims. And so it goes, until there is no one left in the village, only the living dead and the dead." The doctor spread his hands. "You see how it is?"

Tilney looked away. "It sounds horrible," he said quietly.

"It is," the doctor stated. "And it is much worse if you have seen it with your own eyes, I assure you. Now you know why I must hunt the vampire."

"Hunt those vampires, then," said Tilney. "Hunt the monsters—but not Mr. Barksdale."

"The vampire hound is no different."

"He is," Tilney insisted.

Dr. Van Detta gave him a look of pity. "I admire your loyalty, Mr. Potts. Loyalty is a fine quality in anyone. I only wish you had given your loyalty to something more deserving."

"I would give my life for Mr. Barksdale," Tilney declared.

"I sincerely hope that will not be necessary," the doctor replied. He stood up and walked to the window. With his sleeve, he rubbed a layer of dirt from one of the panes. "I must apologize for these accommodations," he said, sweeping his arm around the room. "They are a bit spartan, I'm afraid, but it was the best I could do on short notice. Nothing like Mr. Barksdale's town house in Mayfair, I suppose?"

Tilney's face remained immobile.

"Belgravia? Regent's Park?" the doctor asked.

The rat's expression did not change.

Van Detta shrugged. "Well, you cannot blame me for trying. Fortunately, I no longer need to seek out your master; now he will come to me. In the meantime, let us all be as comfortable as possible. Later, the bear will bring us some tea. You English must have your tea." The doctor took his place on the crate once again. He drew a book from his coat pocket, opened it, and began to read silently.

The ropes that bound Tilney's arms were beginning to bite into his skin. "I'd be a lot more comfortable without these bonds," he said to the doctor.

Dr. Van Detta raised his eyes from his book. "I must remind you, Mr. Potts—you are a prisoner. You must expect certain inconveniences."

Chuggers sat on a barrel in the alley. With the claw on his right forefinger, he carved a letter into the wood.

"There you has it," he said, finishing with a flourish. "That is my mark: C for *Chuggers*."

Slatkin leaned against the bricks, his arms folded across his chest. "I'm surprised it ain't a S," he sneered.

"S?" said the bear. "Why would it be a S? Is you saying I don't know how to spell my own name?"

"You don't know how to spell your own name," the ferret snapped. "But the S would stand for *spy*."

"*Spy*?" Chuggers repeated.

"*Spy*. S-P-I-E. *Spy*," said the ferret.

The bear squinted at Slatkin with his good right eye. "I ain't following you."

"Let me put it to you more plain-like. How long you been spying on me for Toby Thigpen?"

The bear studied Slatkin for a moment. Then he looked down at his stomach, as if the answer were somehow written there. He scratched. Finally, he replied, "Since he asked me."

"You said you was my friend," Slatkin grumbled bitterly.

"I is your friend."

"Then why you working for Toby?"

"Why you working for the doctor?" the bear answered. "Because Toby told you to, that's why. Well, do you think you is the only one who owes Toby money?"

The ferret narrowed his eyes, mulling this over. "It still ain't right," he said. "Friends ain't supposed to spy on friends."

"And I suppose you'd rather have one of Toby's toughs digging them coins out of your hide with a knife?"

"Of course I wouldn't," said Slatkin.

"Well, if it weren't for me," Chuggers stated, "them thugs would be tanning your hide by now. That black bird of Toby's was all for making an example of you, but I told 'em this case we was working on was bound to bring in plenty of bob, so Toby agreed to lay off for a while. So you see, I weren't spying on you, Slatkin; I were looking out for you."

The ferret was silent. He turned his attention to the street. Two men balanced on a high scaffold, painting a building nearby. The men had paint buckets in their left hands and brushes in their right. They slapped long streaks of white paint on the building. Every time they moved, the scaffold shook. But it did not fall down, and the men did not fall off. Still, it made the ferret shudder just to watch them.

I hates that bear, Slatkin thought. *I hates him, and I hates my whole stupid, messy, mixed–up, noisy, no–good life. Seems like every day is a battle to survive, and I am worn out with fighting. All I wants is to fill my belly and lie down and not have the world bother me for about a hundred years. That's all I want, because I am just . . . tired. I am so tired, I ain't even got the starch to stay mad at this here thickheaded, spying bear.*

"I don't see why you is angry at me," said Chuggers.

"Of course you don't see," Slatkin replied. "You don't see nothing, good eye or no. You might as well have a cane and a tin cup."

"I done that," Chuggers recalled, "until a real blind beggar found me out and whacked me with his stick. You going to stay angry for long?"

"Yes."

"How long?"

"How should I know?" the ferret muttered. "A hundred years, maybe."

The bear bobbed his heavy head. "All right," he said. "As long as it's not forever."

After that, neither of them spoke for several minutes. Finally, the ferret coughed and asked, "What if this case don't bring in plenty of bob?"

"Then Toby's boys will be looking for both of us."

"Both of us?" said Slatkin.

"'Course," Chuggers replied. "After all, we is partners, ain't we?"

XVI

Bramstoke Wharf

The packing crate in the empty flat was there for a reason. Tilney discovered the reason later that night, when he was gagged once more and placed in the bottom of the crate. "It's a short journey, sir," said the doctor, bending over the crate. "Remain quiet and enjoy the ride." The lid came down. Blackness closed around Tilney. He tensed. It was like his old nightmare of being buried in the coal. He bit down hard on the gag, fighting back the panic that was swelling in his chest. *Stay calm,* he told himself. *Stay calm and breathe. If you can't see, concentrate on what you can hear.*

They were carrying him now.

"Hold your end up," the ferret grumbled.

"I is holding my end up," the bear replied. "It's your end which is sagging."

"'Cause now you is holding your end too high!" the ferret complained.

"How am I supposed to know what to do, when you can't make up your mind?" the bear demanded.

"Shut up and place the crate on the handcart," the doctor ordered.

The crate landed with a thump that jarred Tilney. There was

a creaking sound, and then the cart was moving, rattling over the pavement.

"You is pushing too fast," said the ferret.

"I am?" the bear's voice answered.

"Can't you tell I is practically running?"

"I was just trying to keep up with the doctor," said the bear. "Besides which, you is on my blind side. But now that you has informed me, I shall be happy to slow down."

Tilney felt the pace of the cart slacken.

"Why are you slowing down?" That was the doctor's voice. "We must reach our meeting place well ahead of the hound."

The bear grunted, and the cart sped up again.

"I ain't so sure I like that doctor," the bear muttered.

"On that we is agreed," the ferret said, puffing.

After that, there was very little to be heard from Tilney's abductors, except for the grunting of the bear and the coughing and cursing of the ferret. Not that it mattered, for Tilney was too distracted to listen sharp. As the rigid wheels of the cart encountered London's irregular pavement, the little rat felt like a cricket ball being continually swatted. It was all he could do to keep his brains from being dashed out against the sides of the crate.

A short time later—though it seemed a long time to the rat—Tilney heard church bells chime the half hour. *Those are the bells of St. Magnus Martyr, or my name is not Tilney Potts*, he thought. Next, the rank smell of the river slipped under the lid of the wooden crate. *Yes, we are near the waterfront.* Nearby were the streets where Tilney had grown up. Nan's home was not far away. *I wish I might see Nan again*, Tilney thought. *And Fred, and the children. And if Father happened to be there . . .*

The cart came to a halt. The crate was lifted off. A door opened and shut. Abruptly, one end of the crate was tilted up, so that Tilney was nearly standing on his head.

He was being carried up stairs.

"Don't know why we couldn't do this at the flat," Tilney

heard the ferret moan. "No, instead we has to—Ouch! Watch my fingers, will ya?"

"Sorry," said the bear.

"'Stead, we has to haul this rat—*oomph*—who must have lead in his boots, through the streets and up these stairs, like we was beasts of burden. Ow! You bear-brained oaf! You trying to crack my ribs?"

"How can I help it," the bear replied, "when you is all the time stopping without warning, and I can't see because the doctor won't wait with the light? I already knocked my head against a post, didn't I?"

"Then I is sorry for the post!"

"I don't know why you is complaining," the bear shot back. "I has to take most of the weight, plus the doctor's bag. How come you don't never carry the bag?"

"Because my shoulders is narrow, and your shoulders is as thick as your head."

There was a pause. "Well, all right, then," said the bear. "As long as there's a reason."

Tilney couldn't help smiling at the discomforts being suffered by his captors. He tried to add to their difficulties by imagining that he was a very fat rat made of solid stone.

Each flight of stairs was followed by a turn. Tilney measured their progress upward. One floor, two floors, three floors. At the fourth floor, the climbing stopped.

"Down there," said the doctor. "Near the loading doors."

"My arms is about to drop off," groaned the ferret.

"Should that happen, the honest citizens of London would thank me for it," the doctor commented.

Moments later, the crate came to rest. The lid was removed. The bear reached in, lifted Tilney from the box, and set him on his feet.

Tilney felt like he had risen from the grave. He took a deep breath . . . and was nearly overcome by the sweet, heavy musk of the tropics.

The vast floor of the wharf was lined with row after row of

burlap sacks and wooden barrels, resting now after their long voyages from India, China, Arabia, Malaya, Sumatra, Jamaica, and countless other sun-drenched lands where British traders came to call. There were towers of cinnamon and bastions of sugar, parapets of pepper and bulwarks of tea, all piled to the rafters of the high ceiling. The scent of foreign lands was so powerful, Tilney half expected to find palm trees, rather than pillars, supporting the roof.

"Can I take off the gag?" Chuggers said to the doctor. "I don't like looking at his face that way."

"If you like," Van Detta replied. "Should he shout, no one will hear. The building is empty at this hour, except for a watchman. And he has orders to ignore us."

They were in the central aisle of the fourth floor of the wharf. The aisle was about fifteen feet wide, flanked on both sides by pillars that ran the length of the building, from the loading doors on the river side to the stairwell on the street side. Lamps were affixed to several of the pillars. The doctor lit the lamps, creating a glowing corridor between the walls of cargo.

Van Detta marched to the loading doors and pulled them open. He stood beneath the arched doorway, the night air on his face, his toes on the edge of the platform, one short step from a straight drop to the water far below.

Jump, Tilney wished. *Go to the devil, and leave us all in peace.*

But the doctor swung away from the edge. Drawing his watch from his waistcoat pocket, he checked the time.

"Ferret!" he barked.

Still sweating from the climb, Slatkin lay sprawled upon a mattress of spice sacks. Wearily, he lifted his head. "What you want now?" he said.

"Take the rat over there by the windows, and stay out of sight until I summon you. When you are called, do exactly as I command. And keep an eye on Mr. Potts; our enterprise depends on him."

The ferret heaved himself off the sacks. Hooking a finger

over the rope across Tilney's chest, the ferret led the rat into the shadows between the stacks of goods and the windows overlooking the river.

Dr. Van Detta then addressed Chuggers. "You will take a position by the windows on the other side of the loading door. If the vampire attacks, I may require your fighting skills . . . whatever those may be."

"You ain't never seen a fighter like me," boasted Chuggers, raising his fist. "Why, I once fought five sailors at the same time. I'da beat 'em, too, if I hadn't got my head stuck in that spittoon." Sticking out his chin, he marched off to his place.

Tilney leaned his forehead against a window overlooking the river.

"Have a seat," said Slatkin, as he plopped himself down on a sack of tea. "Take a rest. I sure needs one." He scratched his throat. "Actually, I needs a lot more than that."

"What do you need?" asked Tilney. "You know I can help you."

"Can you now?" the ferret scoffed. "I'd say that's a rather grand statement from someone who's tied up like a Christmas pudding."

"Nonetheless, I'm always willing to do a favor for a friend."

Slatkin laughed. "In that case, friend, would you mind doing a bit of hocus-pocus and making me disappear? 'Cause I needs to be elsewhere than here, for starters."

"I'll work on it," said Tilney.

The ferret grunted. "You do that, little rat. Anyways, with any luck, we'll all be on our way home soon."

"What does the doctor have in mind?" asked Tilney.

"Why you asking me?" Slatkin replied. He lay back with his paws behind his head. "The doctor don't tell me nothing. 'Course, I do know he is most anxious to get his hands on your Mr. Barksdale. Maybe this will be the night."

"We mustn't allow any harm to come to Mr. Barksdale," said Tilney.

"We mustn't, hey? Well, I don't wish the hound no harm, but I don't exactly see how we can prevent it, neither."

"There must be something you can do."

"Me?!" said Slatkin. "Why do it have to be me? Who am I to be doin' the right thing? Ain't I a thief? Ain't I a housebreaker? Ain't I a desperado of the worst sort? How you gonna change that? Nobody looks out for Slatkin, I can tell you; why should I have to look out for anyone else? Your master ain't my problem, and neither is you. I got problems enough of my own. All I got to do tonight is make sure no harm don't come to myself. And that's an end on it!" The ferret yanked his cap down over his face and clapped his arms across his bony chest.

Disappointed by Slatkin's rebuff, Tilney looked out the dirty window. The sun had nearly set. Mist was rising off the river. The lamps of Southwark flickered on the far shore.

The rat tried to move his arms. After hours of being bound to his sides, they were stiff and aching. Some of the old pain had returned to his injured shoulder. He felt helpless—so helpless that he was running out of hope.

"My father and brothers worked this wharf," Tilney recalled, "after the colliers had all moved downriver."

The ferret said nothing.

"Father wanted me to work on the river, too," Tilney went on. "But it wasn't the life for me." He sighed. "Maybe I should have tried harder. Maybe none of this trouble would have occurred, if I had stayed on the river."

The ferret peeked out from under his hat. "My dad wanted me to be a clerk," he said.

Tilney turned around. "I gather you had other plans."

"Made me go to school, learn my letters and numbers," Slatkin said. "Told me I had to practice with the pen, so's I could write a good hand and get a good job in an office." He chuckled. "Can you imagine me, a clerk? Sitting at a desk every day, all respectable-like, with white collar and cuffs? Ain't sure

I wouldn't rather go to prison. Ain't sure I won't," he added.

"I'll bet you could have done it, though," Tilney told him. "Become a clerk, I mean. You could have lived a different life."

The ferret shrugged. "Who knows? Maybe. Too bad we don't get to try out different lives, hey? Get to choose the one we like?"

"Was your father a clerk?" the rat inquired.

"My dad? No, my dad worked in the Millwall shipyards. Made boilers. Helped make the boilers for the *Great Eastern* herself."

"You don't say."

"Largest ship in the world she was," Slatkin declared. "My dad told me about the making of it many a time. I reckon that great gray hull were quite a sight to behold." The ferret smiled wanly, remembering. "Oh, my dad were proud of that work. And the money were good, too, what with the union and all. But it couldn't last, of course. It never lasts."

"What happened?"

Slatkin removed his hat and spun it slowly on his finger. "Everything changed. One day he had good work, the next day he didn't. One day the yards was full of new ships, the next day the yards was empty. Whole shipbuilding business sank faster than you can say, 'God save the Queen.'

"My dad looked for another position, o' course—him and the tens o' thousands of others that was thrown out of the yards. So you can guess what kind of luck he had. Tried every factory and boatyard from Greenwich to Windsor. Finally, he wound up with all the other unemployed in this town, begging for a day's work on the docks."

"My father did the same," Tilney said.

"Then you know what it's like," the ferret replied. "I hate to admit it, but I even tried the docks a few times myself." He leaned over and spat on the floor. "I never seen a more disgraceful exhibition. Thousands o' desperate souls, all pushing up to the gates like the docks was Heaven and the foreman St. Peter hisself. Young ones climbing over the old. Everyone shouting for the foreman's attention." He scowled. "Shameful is what it is. Humiliating. I can tell you it put me off honest labor forever. Of course"— and here he smiled—"it weren't a total loss. There was a few men in the crowd with a copper or two in their pockets, who found that them same pockets was empty after they rubbed elbows with a certain ferret."

"Did your father ever find steady work?"

"Not likely," said Slatkin. "He weren't young, you know. Pretty soon, the dock foreman wouldn't even look his way. I guess he could've gone north, to the big new shipyards on the Tyne and the Clyde. But it ain't so easy to leave your home and go to a strange place like Scotland. So he stayed here, tried different things, none of 'em worth much. In the end, he were a sandwich-board man. Out of doors all day, in all weathers—it pretty much finished him."

"I'm sorry to hear it," Tilney offered.

"No need," Slatkin replied. "His story ain't so different from a million others. But it did teach me one thing: there's easier ways to get money . . . if you don't mind the risks."

"Don't you ever get tired of stealing, though?"

"Sometimes. But then, I also gets tired of starving."

"Still, it's wrong," Tilney argued.

"Of course it is," said Slatkin, with a hurt look. "Think I don't know it? Think I wasn't taught right from wrong? I know I'm a thief. But at least I'm an honest thief. I don't steal a thousand jobs, then hide behind the door of the Carlton Club while I tally up my profits. There's worse criminals than me living in them fancy houses I burgle."

"That doesn't make it right," Tilney insisted.

"Well, you ain't the judge," Slatkin snapped. "And besides"— he placed the battered hat back on his head, cocking it over one eye—"it takes all kinds to make a world. Without the likes of me, all them constables, watchmen, and jailers would be nothin' but filthy beggars."

XVII

A Walk in the Dark

Barksdale had left the Hodge residence and returned straightway to Harker Lane. Without removing his hat and coat, he went directly upstairs to the drawing room. There he prowled around the furniture, his paws clasped tightly behind his back, his ears twitching with agitation.

The hound had decisions to make, yet his mind was like a flock of blackbirds, wheeling and diving but refusing to settle anywhere. He stopped dead in the middle of the room, placing his paws on either side of his head.

"You must get hold of yourself," he said. "You must do things one at a time, until you have completed them all." He checked the clock on the mantel. He had told Fred that he would meet him at nine o'clock. That left a little more than three hours.

He decided to have a bath first. "Whatever happens, you might as well look like a gentleman," he told himself. He hurried to the bedroom, where he threw his hat and coat on the bed, then began filling the tub in the adjoining bathroom. He hastily undressed, dropping his clothes on the floor.

No, he thought. *Mustn't leave a mess for Potts.* Scooping the clothes from the carpet, he laid them neatly on the bed.

When the bath was ready, Barksdale stepped into the

water—and was so shocked by the chill that he nearly leaped out of the tub. "Of course it's cold, you fool," he told himself through clenched teeth. "Potts isn't here to heat the boiler!" Dancing in the frigid water, the hound debated whether to forgo his bath. *Good grooming never won a fight,* he thought.

Moving slowly, Barksdale stooped until he could splash himself. Snatching up the soap, he scrubbed his fur vigorously. When he felt clean enough, he splashed more water to rinse and stood up, trembling with cold. He shook the water from his fur, then hopped out of the bath and into a towel, which he pulled tight around his shivering body. He sat on a stool with the towel around him until the chill had been flushed from his legs. Then he drained the bath. He even wiped the hairs from the tub.

After he was thoroughly dried and brushed, the hound put on a clean undervest and drawers. He slipped into a white shirt, attaching fresh collar and cuffs. From his dresser he selected a black tie, which he fashioned into a bow at his throat. He opened the armoire, which contained his newest suit—coat, pants, and waistcoat, all in black. He put them on. Finally, he slipped into his boots. Checking his appearance in the mirror, the hound saw that he was every inch a proper English gentleman, ready for an evening at the club, the music hall, or the theater. "Unfortunately, your evening will not be half so pleasant," Barksdale warned his reflection.

The hound's last act before he left the bedroom was to take the picture of his mother from the dressing table and place it in the inside pocket of his coat, close by his heart.

Barksdale now moved to the drawing room, where he took a metal strongbox from a desk drawer and placed it on the desktop. Within the box were a stack of bank notes and several cloth bags filled with coins. Barksdale counted the bank notes out onto the desk blotter. He recounted them, then folded the currency together and placed it, too, in his coat pocket.

Sovereigns, crowns, shillings, and pence clinked and rasped

as the hound emptied the sacks of coins onto the desk. Like a Chinese merchant working an abacus, Barksdale flicked the coins around the desktop with his fingertips, until he had isolated the gold sovereigns. These he quickly tallied.

"Thirty-seven," he murmured, with a frown. "It hardly seems enough." Yet where could he get more? The bank was shut. His solicitor, Mr. Church, would loan him additional sums, but there was no time for a trip to the solicitor's home in Regent's Park.

"This will have to do," said the hound. He swept the sovereigns into one of the sacks and was about to close the mouth of the bag with a length of twine when he hesitated. *What are you hoping for? No sense in saving your coppers now,* he told himself. With that, he scooped the rest of the coin heap into the sack and tied it shut. He dropped the heavy parcel into his coat, where the weight threatened to tear through the bottom of the pocket.

There remained two letters to be written. The first was to Mr. Church. In a swift but steady hand, Barksdale explained to the solicitor what he was about to do. He hoped his old protector and advisor would understand. He also expressed his gratitude to Mr. Church for his many years of excellent counsel and service.

"Please see to it that all bequests are made promptly and in full," Barksdale wrote. "I am especially anxious that there should be no lapse in funding for the Children's Establishment in Limehouse and the Home for Incurable Children in Maida Vale. They have never enough for all the good they do. As always, these donations are to be made anonymously."

When he tried to compose the second letter, the hound discovered that his words would not flow. He stared at the blank sheet of stationery. Several times he dipped the pen in the ink, but before he could transfer the ink to the paper, he had changed his mind, frustrated and embarrassed by the inadequacy of his sentiments. For a while, Barksdale simply gazed out of the drawing room window, watching the light retreat from the sky like the tide pulling away from the shore. Finally, he scratched these words on the paper:

My Dear Mr. Potts:
    Never forget that I am, and shall always be, your most grateful friend,
                        Barksdale

The hound read it over several times. Then he blotted the ink and folded the sheet in half.

Barksdale checked the clock; it was time to go.

The sack of coins was so heavy that the hound had to tilt his right shoulder downward in order to keep his balance. "I should have used two sacks," he told himself, "one in each pocket." It seemed pointless to make a change, however. The discomfort was slight, and he would not have to endure it long.

Barksdale placed the letter for Tilney on the table in the entrance hall. He laid the letter to Mr. Church beside it. Potts would see that Mr. Church's letter reached the solicitor's office in the City. Potts would see to everything.

Moments later, the vampire hound shut the door on 1 Harker Lane. He did not bother to unlock the front gate. He simply went up and over the wall. And he did not look back.

The bells in the elegant round tower of St. Mary-le-Bow were tolling nine as Nan Hodge admitted Mr. Barksdale to her home. Nan's father was seated by the fire. Fred stood off to the side, buttoning and rebuttoning his waistcoat.

"Tilney's cousins have been watching Bramstoke Wharf," old Mr. Potts reported to the hound. "They've seen no sign of my son. A short while ago, however, a ferret and a bear was seen delivering a package to the wharf."

"That'd be the 'committee men' what spoke to me, I'll bet," said Fred.

"They was with another," the old rat continued. "A beefy sort of fella, dressed like a gent. They went in, and they ain't come out."

"I trust that your lookouts were not detected," said Barksdale.

"I told you, we rats have a talent for staying out of sight."

"I sincerely appreciate all of your efforts, Mr. Potts. I'm certain your son will be even more grateful."

The old rat snorted. "For your own, you do everything you can," he said gruffly. He rubbed a gnarled forefinger under his nose.

"Are you ready then, Fred?" Barksdale asked.

Fred jerked his head up, his eyebrows pointing skyward like the raised spans of the new Tower drawbridge. "Is it time?" he said. "Already?"

"I'd like to arrive early," the hound replied, "and take a few minutes to reconnoiter."

"Oh, well, of course," said Fred. He wore the expression of a condemned prisoner who hopes that hanging might not be as bad as it looks.

"Good luck to you, Mr. Barksdale," Nan Hodge said. "Do bring my brother home safe and sound—and my husband, too."

The hound placed his top hat over his heart. "You will have them back, Mrs. Hodge. I promise you."

Nan helped her husband into his coat. She gave him a quick kiss on the cheek. "You mind what Mr. Barksdale says," she lectured Fred. "And you stay out of trouble. Remember what I told you."

"Aye, and remember what I told you," Ephraim Potts warned.

"Don't you worry, Nan," Fred replied. "I won't be getting no heroic ideas." From the paleness of Fred's complexion, it appeared that he meant exactly what he said.

Minutes later, Barksdale and Fred were walking east on Cannon Street. Neither of them had spoken since they had left the rat's house. Fred was muzzled by his visions of what might happen that night. The hound, on the other hand, believed that he already knew the future, and he had no desire to think about it; indeed, thinking might prevent him from doing what needed to be done. He was, instead, concentrating on the sensations of the moment: the way the pavement pressed against the soles of his feet; how the air brushed the fur on his cheeks; how the coin sack in his left coat pocket bounced heavily against his hip.

Fred cleared his throat. "Sir," he said tentatively, "are these very desperate characters that we're dealing with tonight?"

Barksdale took a moment before answering. "I shouldn't call them 'desperate,' Fred," he replied. "They are, however, quite serious."

"Serious," Fred repeated, biting his lip.

"Not that it should concern you, Fred," Barksdale assured the rat. "If all goes the way I think it will, you won't be dealing with these characters at all."

Fred exhaled audibly. "I'm glad of that, Mr. Barksdale. I mean, not that I wouldn't be quick to mix it up with them fellows, if I was called upon."

"I'm certain you would fight like a tiger," said the hound.

"I once caught a weasel trying to burgle the shop," Fred recounted. "Conked him on the head with a round of Cheddar. He run like a rabbit . . . or, at least, like a scared weasel."

"Good for you, Fred."

"'Course, Nan said I ought to have hit him with something besides my stock. In truth, it didn't do the cheese much good. Nor me, neither. After that, I was so nervous, I didn't sleep for two weeks."

"I still think it was a bold thing to do," said the hound. "I'm certain that many a man who has won the Victoria Cross has lost sleep over the deed."

A vision of Queen Victoria presenting him with a medal caused Fred to straighten his shoulders. It also gave him the courage to question the hound further.

"Sir, if you don't mind my asking . . ."

"What is it, Fred?"

"Is there any truth to the tale that you is some sort of Indian maharaja?"

Barksdale chuckled. "Who in the world told you that?"

"I got it from my kids, who had the story from their Uncle Tilney."

"Mr. Potts has a most lively imagination, Fred. I'm afraid that I have never set foot on the Indian subcontinent, nor, to the best of my knowledge, have any of my relatives. We may be mysterious, but we are not from the East."

Fred was clearly disappointed. "Then I suppose that bit about the card-playing cobra is also a fairy tale?"

Barksdale was uncertain how to respond. He liked Fred and did not wish to shatter all his illusions. In addition, the hound did not wish to make Tilney out a liar. After a moment's hesitation, he said, "The cobra? Oh, that part about the cobra is perfectly true. We play cards nearly every evening."

"And he really looks like the Prince of Wales?"

Good heavens! thought Barksdale. *Potts must be a tale-spinner worthy of the Arabian Nights!* "He is the spitting image of His Royal Highness," he stated. "But then, he is a spitting cobra, after all."

"Imagine that," said Fred, with wonder.

"Yes, it takes some imagining," the hound remarked.

By now, they had passed the intersection of Cannon and King William streets. Another turn, and they were approaching the Monument, Sir Christopher Wren's memorial to the Great Fire of 1666, which had begun in nearby Pudding Lane.

"Ever climbed up there, sir?" asked Fred, pointing to the top of the two-hundred-foot column.

"No, I have not."

"They say it's a marvelous view of the city, sir. Of course, I never been up there myself. I ain't so well off that I can pay tuppence just for a view."

"Who knows, Fred? Maybe you'll get your chance someday.

By the way, have you ever been to the top of Cleopatra's Needle?"

"No, sir. Have you?"

"Once, recently."

"Is it a sight worth seeing, sir?"

"It gives a fair view of the river."

Fred was silent for a moment. "Funny thing," he said. "I never even knew you could climb to the top of Cleopatra's Needle."

"You can, Fred," the hound replied. "But you must have a good reason."

Now the bells of St. Magnus Martyr struck half past.

"We're nearly there, aren't we, Fred?"

"Nearly," said the rat. "Do you mind if I ask one more question, sir? It's a trifling thing. I almost hate to bring it up."

"Go on," Barksdale replied.

"Well, sir, Her Majesty's Diamond Jubilee is not so far off, and I was wondering: Do you think Her Majesty would appreciate a bust of her royal self carved from cheese?"

The hound gave a series of small coughs.

"Is you all right, sir?"

"It must be the night air," Barksdale explained. "I'm not used to it."

"It can play havoc with a fellow's wind," Fred observed.

"Yes, well, in answer to your question, I think Her Majesty would be most appreciative of any token which is sincerely offered by one of her loyal subjects."

"I am grateful for your advice, sir," Fred replied. "Most grateful. 'Course, my Nan may have an opinion of her own on this matter. Which opinion may settle the matter once and for all, no matter what you or I might think, if you'll pardon my saying it, sir."

"Your wife is most sensible," said Barksdale, "as I'm certain you know."

"I knows it, sir. And if I forgets, Nan is good about reminding me."

Another turn, and their destination was in sight. Bramstoke Wharf stood fast among the other wharves and warehouses that lined the river like a row of biscuit tins on a grocery shelf. The wharf's many ranks of windows were all shut in darkness, except for a dim glow behind a window shade on the fourth floor.

Suddenly, another rat popped up at Fred's elbow.

"Hey! You nearly frighted me to death!" hissed Fred. "I wish you wouldn't sneak up on a bloke like that."

"Sorry, Fred," said the other rat. "Sometimes we just can't help it."

Fred introduced the newcomer to the hound. He was Nigel, a second cousin to Tilney.

"Them three as went in, they're still in there," Nigel reported. "At least, we ain't seen them come out. But we ain't seen Tilney, neither."

"They said he would be here at ten o'clock," Barksdale replied. "I think we may trust them on that point."

"Uncle Ephraim told us we wasn't to go inside," Nigel continued, "though some of the boys was most eager. We could've done it, you know."

"I'm certain you could," the hound acknowledged. "But you were wise to heed your uncle's advice. To do otherwise might have endangered Tilney."

"I had a report from Cousin Alf," Nigel added. "He's been watching the river side of the wharf from London Bridge. He says the loading doors to the fourth floor is open, and there's a lamp shining inside. He's seen a gent standing in the doorway, but that's all."

"Anything else I should know?"

"There's a fat old watchman on the ground floor, but he's so sound asleep, you couldn't wake him with a train whistle."

"I appreciate the information," said the hound. "I'm most grateful for everything you have done for your cousin."

"No bother," said Nigel. "Besides, we has to look out for each other, don't we? Who else would look out for rats, except other rats?" With a tip of his cap, he slipped away into the darkness.

Keeping to the shadows, Barksdale led Fred to a doorway opposite Bramstoke Wharf.

"I have two directives for you, Fred," said Barksdale, in a low but earnest tone. "The first is this: You must wait here—exactly here—for one hour after I leave you. If Tilney does not exit the wharf by eleven o'clock, then it is likely that my efforts have failed, and you must gather all the help you can and try to free Tilney in your own way."

"I'll do that, sir."

"And here is the second directive." Barksdale removed the sack of coins from his coat pocket and handed it to Fred. The parcel was so heavy, it nearly slipped through the rat's paws.

"What's this?" asked Fred. From the weight and the shape, it appeared to be a bag full of money.

"You are to have this," said Barksdale. "You and your family. It is my gift to you, to use as you wish. Climb to the top of the Monument, if you like. It is too little, but it is my way of thanking you for all you have done."

"But . . . but we ain't done nothing," Fred objected.

"You have shared your lives with me, though you never knew it," Barksdale explained. "You have given me a family of my own, and that is a great gift. Good luck to you and yours, Fred. Remember my orders."

Before Fred could stop him, before the rat could stammer out his confusion, before he could attempt to return the money, the hound was gone. Fred stood alone in the inky shadows, grasping what felt like a small fortune. He didn't know what to think. Should he be overjoyed? Should he be insulted? Should he be worried about carrying such a treasure through the streets?

In the end, of course, only one thing mattered. "What's Nan going to think?" whispered Fred.

XVIII

Dealing with the Doctor

No one, not even Tilney's cousins, saw Barksdale clamber up the brick face of the wharf; but then, who would look for a gentleman climbing a building as if it were a ladder? With his arms extended like a tightrope walker, the hound stepped lightly along the peak of the roof to the river side of the wharf. He peered over the edge. Two stories below, the loading doorway was still open and glowing with light. Far below that, the leaden river wound silently through the city.

Barksdale fished his watch from his waistcoat pocket. *Nearly ten,* he noted. *I wonder where I shall be at eleven?* He snapped the watch shut and returned it to its place. Leaning over the edge of the roof, he placed his left paw firmly against the façade of the wharf. He did the same with the right. Then, like a fly, he started headfirst down the side of the building.

Unfortunately, the hound had forgotten about his hat. As he started down, the topper pitched from his head. Barksdale grabbed for it with his left paw. In that same instant, he knew he had made a serious mistake. Reaching for the hat, he lost his balance. His right paw came away from the bricks, and he fell.

All for a hat? he asked himself, as he plunged downward.

He might have plummeted to the river—plummeted to his

death, perhaps—had it not been for the crane projecting from the wall just below him. This was the derrick used for hoisting cargo in and out of the wharf. To his utter astonishment, Barksdale now crashed facedown onto the arm of the crane. It knocked the wind out of him, but he managed to wrap his arms and legs around the steel beam and hang on.

The hound lay motionless for several minutes. The steel was cool and hard against his muzzle. When his heart stopped pounding and he could breathe once more, he slowly sat up. His ribs were sore, and his right cheek had been battered, but he was otherwise unharmed. He checked his coat pocket for the picture of his mother. Luckily, it was still there and had not been damaged. His watch dangled by its chain. He scanned the river below, but even with his keen night vision, he could detect no sign of his hat. Perhaps some boatman would fish it from the water and wonder about the gent who once wore it. *And wouldn't he like to know my story?* the hound thought.

Barksdale slid feetfirst off the derrick. Placing his paws securely against the bricks, he descended until he was beside the open doorway. There he waited, clinging to the wall, his coattails waving in the night wind. He cocked his ears, listening. There was no sound within the wharf, except the snoring of the watchman.

The bells of London began to chime the hour. Barksdale drew a deep breath. On the stroke of ten, he swung through the doorway into the light.

Van Detta stood twenty feet away, arms folded across his barrel chest, legs spread wide. The unruly crest of red hair dipped over his right eyebrow.

"I knew we would meet again, Mr. Barksdale."

"Some things cannot be avoided," the hound replied, "no matter how unpleasant they may be." His eyes darted from side to side as he advanced toward the doctor. "Where is my servant?"

"He is nearby."

"Show him to me."

The doctor thrust his right arm forward. "Come no closer, vampire," he warned, "if you wish the rat to remain unharmed."

Barksdale halted. "You said you were willing to trade for Potts. What sort of trade? You'll get nothing from me until I am certain that he will go free."

"Of course," Van Detta agreed. "I promise you a fair exchange."

"I want to see him," Barksdale insisted.

The doctor sighed. "Very well. Slatkin! Chuggers! Bring out the rat."

Barksdale heard movement behind him. Glancing over his shoulder, he saw the ferret and the bear shuffling nervously in front of the open doors. Between them stood Tilney Potts, his arms bound tightly to his sides.

The hound stepped quickly to one side, so that he could speak to his friend without turning his back on his enemy. "Potts, are you all right?"

"I am fine, sir," Tilney replied. "Though I wouldn't mind being able to scratch my nose."

"Untie him," the hound said to the doctor.

Van Detta shook his head. "When we have a deal."

"Untie him now!" Barksdale commanded.

The doctor laughed. "Do you think you are in charge here, vampire?"

With a fierce growl, the hound started toward his foe.

"I swear to you," said Van Detta, pointing a finger at Barksdale. "If you attempt to harm me in any way, if I have anything less than your full cooperation, then my associates will hurl your servant into the river. Is that understood?"

Barksdale backed off. "What do you want?" he said. "Do you want money?" From his pocket he produced a wad of bank notes, which he offered to the doctor. "Eighty-five pounds. That is all I have at the moment. Let Tilney go, and tomorrow morning I will make it five hundred."

At the mention of such a sum, Slatkin stood up straight, and the bear's good eye bulged with amazement.

"Easily said," the doctor replied.

"I give you my word. As soon as the bank opens tomorrow, you shall have five hundred pounds. But Potts must leave with me tonight."

"I'd trust him," Chuggers whispered to the ferret. "He's got a more honest face than that doctor—or you, for that matter."

"Yeah? Well, your face ain't nothin' to swear by," Slatkin muttered.

Barksdale still held the money toward the doctor.

Van Detta scratched his cheek. There was a small pink scar where the hound had cut him. "I am not a wealthy man," he said deliberately. "I do not have the fine life you must have, Mr. Barksdale—you who have five hundred pounds to spare. I have had to fight my way up to where I am." He rubbed his hands together, massaging the battered knuckles. "But"—he tipped his head back proudly—"that does not mean I can be bought. I have a contract stating that I am to rid the world of vampires. That contract is my word. As you would honor your word, so I must honor mine."

Reluctantly, Barksdale slipped the money back into his pocket. "If you won't take money, then what deal have we to make?" he inquired.

"It is a very simple transaction," the doctor stated. "I will trade the rat's life for yours."

This was what the hound had expected all along; still, it staggered him like a blow to the face. "You call that a fair exchange?" he said.

Van Detta spread his hands. "It's the best I can offer. Of course, your life is over, whatever you decide. But you have the chance to save your servant."

"Don't, sir. Don't do it," Tilney pleaded.

The hound hesitated, flexing his claws.

"Ferret, move the rat closer to the doorway," Van Detta ordered.

"No!" shouted Barksdale.

"It's merely an incentive," said the doctor. "Something to help you make up your mind. And allow me to remind you again—if you try anything foolish, Mr. Potts will pay for it."

"Swear to me that you will let him go," Barksdale said.

"Swear to me that you will surrender without a fight," Van Detta countered.

"You mustn't, sir," Tilney begged his master. "Fight him! Save yourself!"

Barksdale looked at his servant—bound, helpless, and closely guarded by the bear and the ferret. His eyebrows lifted, as if to say, "What choice do I have, Potts?"

"Your word, sir," the doctor pressed.

"You have my word," Barksdale replied.

"Good," said Van Detta. "When it is done, I shall release the rat unharmed. Do we have a deal?"

"We have a deal."

Dr. Van Detta clapped his hands loudly, causing Slatkin and Chuggers to jump.

"Ferret," the doctor said, "fetch a rope from my bag and bind the hound to this column." He indicated one of the pillars holding up the roof.

Slatkin hesitated.

"Do as I say!" Van Detta commanded.

"I don't know," said the ferret, twisting his neck anxiously. "I ain't sure I wants to get mixed up in this."

"You're already mixed up in this," the doctor reminded him.

"And I don't like it," the ferret complained. "First, it was just finding this hound. Then it become kidnapping, which I ain't never been involved in nothing like before. Now you is talking about murder. I don't want no part of it."

"You agreed to do this job," Van Detta replied. "But if you

wish to leave now, I will be happy to show you the way. Do you get my meaning?"

"Now, don't go threatening my partner," Chuggers warned.

"And do you know how to swim?" the doctor snarled at the bear.

Chuggers moved his mouth but made no answer. He looked at the ferret.

Head bowed in defeat, Slatkin trudged to the doctor's canvas bag and drew out a coil of rope. He approached the hound. "Sorry about this, Mr. Barksdale," he said dejectedly. "I never meant you no harm, truly. Some of us ain't quite so bad as we seem."

The hound stared above the ferret's head in silence.

Slatkin led Barksdale to the pillar and placed him with his back against it. Still he couldn't bring himself to bind the hound. "It ain't right," he said.

"Get on with it!" cried Van Detta. "I would like to complete my business before the wharf opens tomorrow morning."

Biting his lip, the ferret began passing the rope around the hound's chest.

"Do you have any last requests?" the doctor inquired. "A blindfold, perhaps?"

"There is a portrait in my coat pocket," said the hound. "I should like it to be buried with me."

"Burial is for God-fearing souls," the doctor answered, "not for vampires. No, I have made other arrangements for your body, Mr. Barksdale. There must be nothing left of you— nothing that could ever rise again."

The hound glared at Van Detta in disbelief.

Slatkin stopped what he was doing. "Not even a decent burial? Oh, you is a heartless creature."

"I save my compassion for the vampire's victims," the doctor replied. "Tie him tightly."

The ferret went back to his work, all the while muttering angrily to himself.

"There are several ways to destroy a vampire," the doctor lectured. "You can, for instance, expose a vampire to sunlight. With time and suitable weather, the vampire will crumble into dust. This is a rather slow method of execution, however, and, as Krumpelbeck has shown, it is not guaranteed to be fatal in all cases; so I cannot recommend it. Then there is burning, which has the advantage of being both quick and complete. Unfortunately, for our purposes, a fire is not practical; I have no wish to turn the London waterfront into a raging inferno."

"Very considerate," Slatkin sneered.

"As you are only part vampire, Mr. Barksdale—a point you have always been quick to make—I would guess that you could be dispatched in a more conventional manner, with a bullet or a knife, perhaps. But"—the doctor placed his forefinger against his chin—"would those means kill a vampire like you forever? That is the question. If I had the time, I could perform some interesting experiments in that regard. I might then present the evidence at a symposium of my colleagues. You could do a great service for vampirology, Mr. Barksdale. Would you like that?"

The hound made no remark.

Dr. Van Detta threw up his hands. "Alas, the point is moot; I do not have the time for research. Therefore, I shall resort to the standard method of vampire extermination: a wooden stake through the heart."

"No!" cried Tilney. "It's murder!"

"I would advise you to hold your tongue, Mr. Potts," the doctor threatened. "Some would say that your willingness to serve this monster makes you a partner in his crimes. Do not tempt me to pass judgment upon you."

"You gave me your word," Barksdale growled.

"So I did. Yet who would fault me for breaking a promise to a vampire?"

"You are a liar then, as well as a murderer," said the hound.

"I am a man in a difficult profession," Van Detta countered, his face growing red. "I will keep my word, provided your servant does not interfere. And now, I would like to get on with my business. Ferret, is the hound secure?"

"He ain't going nowheres," Slatkin declared. He tugged at the coils crossing the hound's chest. Then, leaning in close, he whispered, "'Course, I wouldn't trust them knots." Surprise flickered in Barksdale's face, but he remained perfectly still. The ferret returned to his place beside Tilney.

Dr. Van Detta strode to the canvas bag and reached inside. He brought out a wooden stake two feet long and a wooden mallet.

"Tools of the trade," he said, showing them to Barksdale. "Some may prefer gaudier instruments—silver-headed mallets, stakes with gold filigree, jeweled crosses. I am a practical man, however, and these simple tools work just as well as those elegant things, at nothing like the price."

He moved resolutely toward the hound, his fingers opening and closing on the stake. Barksdale flexed his arms against the ropes. Were the knots slipping?

"Do you have anything to say?" Van Detta asked.

Barksdale glared at his captor. "See that you keep your end of the bargain. Else you will never get out of here unharmed."

"An idle threat, given your present situation," the doctor answered. "Mr. Potts, have you anything to add?"

Tilney could barely speak. "I . . . thank you, Mr. Barksdale," he whispered.

The hound nodded. "Good-bye, Potts."

Van Detta pressed the point of the stake to the hound's chest above his heart.

Chuggers looked down at his boots. Slatkin chewed his lower lip.

Tightening his grip on the mallet, the doctor drew back his arm.

Let go! thought Barksdale, straining against his bonds. *Let—*

At which point, Tilney Potts—loyal servant, stouthearted rat—sprang across the wharf and sank his teeth into the doctor's thigh.

The stake flew from Van Detta's hand. Howling with pain and surprise, the doctor whirled about, knocking Tilney to the floor. "You treacherous little rodent," he snarled. "I told you to stay out of it!" He raised the mallet above his head.

Suddenly, Barksdale burst from the ropes. He wrenched the mallet from Van Detta and hurled it aside. Then, seizing the stunned doctor by the collar and the seat of his pants, the hound rushed him toward the open loading doors. "Move!" Barksdale yelled at Slatkin and Chuggers. The two burglars dove out of the way. With a furious growl, the hound flung the doctor through the doorway and into the night air. There was a splash as Van Detta hit the water four stories below.

Breathing hard, Barksdale stood in the archway, looking down at the Thames. The ferret sidled up next to him. "Anyways, it's a dirty river," Slatkin pronounced. He spit over the edge. "That doctor'll fit right in."

"I suppose I should thank you," the hound said.

The ferret made a face. "You suppose you should throw me out after the doctor, you mean. Wouldn't blame you if you did, all the trouble I caused you."

"Still—"

"Forget it," said Slatkin. "I'll consider it a favor if you just let us get out of here alive." He turned to his partner. "Chuggers, help that little fellow up and untie him."

The bear lifted Tilney from the floor and removed his bonds. The rat raised and lowered his arms, slowly working the feeling back into his muscles.

Barksdale walked over to his servant and placed a paw on his shoulder. "I should thank you, too, Potts. Once again, you have come to my rescue."

Tilney blushed. "You couldn't bite that doctor, sir, so I simply did it for you."

"Still, I'm sorry for putting you through this ordeal."

"We're all safe now," the rat said. "Everything will be well again."

Barksdale shook his head. "Things can't go on as they did before. I must speak to you about that."

"What do you mean, sir?" Tilney asked.

"We'll just be off, then," Slatkin interrupted. "Sorry again for all the trouble. Come on, Chuggers." The ferret and the bear tipped their caps and started for the stairs.

"Wait," called Barksdale.

Slatkin shoved his partner toward the exit. "Best get out of here," he whispered, "before that hound starts to balance our account and we comes up short."

"Maybe he wants to reward us," Chuggers suggested.

"For what? Nearly getting him—" Slatkin suddenly stopped speaking.

"What's wrong?" asked the bear.

The ferret pointed to a pile of pepper sacks nearby. There sat Jack the raven, a murderous glint in his eye.

XIX

Fred Ex Machina

Toby Thigpen stepped out of the shadows, followed by the tattooed thug and his knife-wielding companion. The raven left his perch to join them. Flapping his wings awkwardly, he crashed into a barrel and fell to the floor.

"Ha!" cried Toby gleefully. "Did you see that, ferret? Jack flies like a chicken, since you knocked him into that glue. Can't get the sticky stuff off his feathers. Most comical thing I ever saw."

Jack lurched back onto his feet. "Not so comical, boss," he croaked. "Not to me."

"Don't you get testy with me," Toby scolded. "I'm not the one responsible for your predicament."

The raven turned his hateful gaze toward Slatkin. "Skin him, boss," he hissed. "Skin the ferret."

"Keep your plumage on, Jack. We'll get to that."

The pig pushed his shiny top hat onto the back of his head. His button eyes scrutinized Barksdale and Tilney, Slatkin and Chuggers.

"Having a pleasant evening?" he inquired.

"We've had worse," said Slatkin. "How about yourself?"

"Not bad at all," Toby replied. "In fact, it's been rather lucky. Look here." He showed his hat to the ferret. "I was scrounging along the riverbank—you know, looking for scrap metal, wood, bodies, that sort of thing—when the breeze blew this perfectly fine topper right into my trotters. Isn't that funny?"

Barksdale instinctively raised his paw to his bare head.

"That is funny," said Slatkin. "Here I just assumed your boys took it off some poor beggar they robbed and beat up."

The two thugs stared hard at the ferret. Chuggers bent toward his partner's ear. "Could we be a mite more charming, perhaps?" the bear whispered. "I wouldn't mind living a bit longer."

Barksdale spoke up. "I believe that may be my hat, sir."

The boar displayed his crooked yellow smile. "Really, sir? And how would that be?"

"I lost it near the river earlier this evening," Barksdale explained.

"But how do I know this is your hat?"

"My toppers come from Lord and Company in St. James's Street," the hound replied. "If you look inside, I'm sure you'll see the company monogram."

The pig turned the hat toward the lamplight and peered inside. "Well, what do you know?" he said. "'Lord and Company.' Yes, a very fine establishment. I do business with them myself. In fact, many a gent buys his toppers at Lord and Company in St. James's Street. There's no reason to think that this particular hat might be yours."

"I assure you it is, sir," said Barksdale.

Toby shook his head. "No, no, I just can't see my way to your point of ownership, sir. Fate delivered this hat to me, and I will not argue with Fate. And you must agree, the fit is excellent." He placed the hat back on his head. The oversize topper sank down, bending the tips of the pig's pointed ears and nearly covering his eyes.

"It don't fit perfect," said Slatkin. "I can still see your face."

"Mr. Barksdale, this is monstrous," Tilney protested. "That scoundrel is stealing your hat!"

"Let it go, Potts," the hound advised. "This fellow is dangerous. Better to lose the hat and keep our heads."

"You didn't come here to show us your hat," said the ferret. "What you doing here, Toby?"

"Looking after my business, of course," the pig replied.

"Well, this ain't any business of yours—nor your ugly friends, neither."

Infuriated by this remark, Jack hopped swiftly toward Slatkin, aiming to slash his ankles. The ferret easily sidestepped the clumsy bird, then booted him through the legs of the tattooed thug.

"Good shot!" Toby exclaimed. "Right through the hoop. He's got the best of you again, Jack. You should give it up, maybe."

Sprawled on the floor, the raven gave an exasperated squawk but said nothing.

"We was just about to leave," Slatkin told Toby. "So, if you don't mind . . ."

"Maybe you should stay awhile," the pig suggested.

"Then you leave," Slatkin countered. "Like I said, this ain't your business."

"Maybe you're wrong there, Slatkin. Maybe this is very much my business. In the first place, I happen to own this wharf, so you are trespassing on my property. In the second place, I had an arrangement with the doctor—by the way, where is the doctor?"

"He stepped out," said Chuggers.

"And he ain't coming back," Slatkin added.

"I see." The pig's shrewd gaze fell on the open loading doors. "Yes, I believe I take your meaning. In that case, I suppose I must make a deal with Mr. Barksdale here myself."

"I'm afraid I am not acquainted with you, sir," said the hound.

"Nor I with you, sir," the pig replied. "Dr. Van Detta told me little enough about you. And I must say, he searched for you in some very peculiar places. But then, I don't care to know too much about such things. I am more interested in figures than in facts. And I could smell money in the doctor's endeavors, just as surely as a country pig can smell an acorn in a pile of leaves."

"Mr. Barksdale," said Slatkin, "allow me to introduce you to the lowest, meanest, cheatingest son of a sow in all of London."

The pig raised his hat. "Toby Thigpen, sir," he said to Barksdale. "A businessman."

"A crook," the ferret muttered.

"He means it in the most honorable sense," added Chuggers, casting a worried look at his partner.

"What do you want from me, Mr. Thigpen?" the hound inquired.

"Whatever I can get," said the pig. "Jack, what sum were we to receive from Dr. Van Detta for allowing him to conduct business in our city?"

The raven was still lying on his back. Without moving, he answered, "Twenty pounds if he didn't find the hound; twenty-five if he did. Plus one and three to dispose of the remains."

"Excellent, Jack. I am constantly amazed by the capacity of your minuscule brain."

"Twenty pounds?" said Slatkin, astounded. "We was only getting a half crown between us. And that's only if we found Barksdale. Otherwise, we got nought."

"And we done the marching and lifting and listening to that doctor all the time," Chuggers complained. "And what about my head?" He removed his cap and rubbed his paw over his skull.

"If you had anything in your head," Toby observed, "maybe you would know how to make money."

"You is right about that, Toby," said Chuggers, who felt a sudden sharp pain as Slatkin elbowed him in the ribs.

Barksdale cleared his throat. "Tell me what you want, Mr. Thigpen."

"Gladly, Mr. Barksdale." Toby bowed slightly. "I can see that you are a gentleman of good sense," he began, "so you will undoubtedly understand my situation. The doctor was about to enrich me by twenty pounds or more. Unfortunately, it seems he is no longer in a position to pay, so I am out good money that was nearly in my pocket."

"And you would like me to make up the sum," Barksdale concluded.

"Not exactly," said the pig. "I think I would be pleased with a rather larger amount. However, as you have already had the misfortune to lose your hat tonight, my terms will not be harsh. A thousand pounds ought to do it. A thousand pounds, and you and your servant may go on your way."

"You chiseler!" Slatkin spat. "Mr. Barksdale offered the doctor five hundred, but he wouldn't take a penny."

"Van Detta should have studied bank drafts instead of books," Toby replied.

"A thousand pounds," Barksdale said, his ears twitching. "That is a great deal of money, Mr. Thigpen. What if I do not have such a fortune?"

"Any gentleman who can offer five hundred must be able to raise a thousand," the pig asserted.

"And if I refuse to pay?"

Toby indicated the two thugs standing behind him. "My associates will see to it that your bones are never found. That goes for the rat, too."

Barksdale looked down at his servant. Tilney's expression was defiant. "It's blackmail, sir," he whispered. "We can't let him get away with it."

"Where does this leave me and Chuggers?" Slatkin interjected. "We don't want no part of this."

"As for you," said Toby, with a sneer, "I am out of patience with both of you. You're going to the glue factory."

"Glue for you! Glue for you!" the raven cackled. "Ferret's gonna pay!"

Slatkin blinked nervously. "Now, Toby," he argued, his voice trembling, "you know that ain't right. We had a deal. You said I could pay the money back."

"And you told me to keep an eye on Slatkin," Chuggers added. "Well, I done that, didn't I? And I only got one good eye."

The pig dismissed their arguments with a wave of his trotter. "Your time is up, both of you. You're not worth the aggravation." He turned to his henchmen. "Stuff them in a barrel, so we can transport them across the river."

"I won't let you do that," Barksdale growled.

The pig grunted with surprise. "What are they to you, sir? I should think maybe you'd be as happy as I to be rid of them."

"I always did like that hound," Chuggers whispered to the ferret.

"Better listen to him, sir," Slatkin said to Barksdale. "You've had enough trouble already. You'd best not get involved with us."

"At the moment, it seems we are all tangled up together, Mr. Slatkin," the hound replied, "and I see no way of unraveling things. I will not stand by and allow this swine to murder you, just as you would not allow the doctor to murder me."

Slatkin glanced around—at Chuggers, who was watching him intently; at the two thugs, who were beginning to crack their knuckles and roll their muscular shoulders beneath their coats; at Toby, who was polishing Barksdale's topper with a dirty handkerchief; and, lastly, at the hound, who did indeed look like someone ready to battle on the ferret's behalf.

"Well, Mr. Barksdale, I ain't going to let Toby put the screws to you like he done to me and everyone else," Slatkin vowed. "I've had enough and more than enough of bullies like him. And that's an end on it!"

"Is you serious?" Chuggers asked.

"Dead serious," the ferret replied.

The bear scratched his jaw. "That's what I was afraid of."

Toby gave a snort of disgust. "I am disappointed in you, Slatkin. I never expected this sort of bravado from someone of your experience. You used to be more reasonable."

"Foolish ferret!" the raven croaked with delight. "It's glue for you!"

"You mean I used to be afraid to spit in your eye, like I should've done," the ferret told Toby.

The pig shook his head. "So what am I supposed to do? Let all of you go, just like that? Congratulate you on your newfound backbone, pat you on the head, and wish you Godspeed? And get nothing for it? Nothing for my trouble? Is that what you expect?" He snorted again. "If all my deals went like that, I should soon have nothing to deal with. Someone else would be sitting in my chair, and I would be lying on a silver platter with an apple stuffed in my mouth."

The raven tittered.

"Don't you be thinking about that, Jack," the pig warned. The boar placed his trotters on his thick hips and leaned forward. "No, no, ferret. No, Mr. Barksdale. I did not become the pig I am by letting others get the better of me. No, I will have some profit from you, living or dead."

"Skin 'em, boss!" urged the raven.

"It's all I can do, Jack," the pig replied. "We must close the book on these fellows, I'm afraid."

Toby motioned for the thugs to step forward. "Don't make a mess of it," he told them quietly. "I have valuable property in here."

His henchmen nodded and pushed up their sleeves. The tattooed man produced a blackjack from his coat pocket. His partner brandished his knife.

"Get behind me, Potts," said Barksdale, keeping an eye on the thugs. "Run when I tell you."

Tilney snatched up the stake Dr. Van Detta had dropped on the floor. "I'm not leaving without you, sir," he declared, wielding the stake like a javelin.

"Look at the little rat," mocked the tattooed man. "He thinks he's a blinkin' Zulu!"

His partner laughed, then spat on his knife, wiping the blade on his thigh.

"Here, Slatkin." Chuggers picked up the doctor's mallet and handed it to the ferret. "See if you can't raise a few lumps on their ugly knobs."

"What you going to do?" asked Slatkin.

The bear crouched with his fists in front of his face. "A bit o' paw, a bit o' claw," he snarled. "I ain't afraid of them two mugs. I'll shred 'em like they was paper."

"Paper don't carry no knife," muttered the ferret, grasping the mallet with both paws. He glanced back over his shoulder at the loading doors, which remained open to the night sky. "Maybe we should take our chances with the river," he wondered aloud.

"Go on, if you like," Chuggers replied, "but count me out. I ain't no swimmer. If I go out that door, I'll drop like a anchor. Besides, you ain't the only one who's tired of bein' pushed around. Everyone does it to me—constables, Toby, that doctor . . . even you."

"Me?" the ferret said in disbelief. "When do I push you around?"

"Only all the time."

"You don't know—"

"Oh, it's all right," Chuggers said. "I don't mind so much when you does it. That's just the way some friendships is."

Slatkin looked once more at the doorway. Then he looked at the bear. "Well," he decided, "with my luck, I'd probably jump right down the smokestack o' some steamer." He took a few swings with the mallet.

Toby stamped his boot. "Why aren't they dead already?" he complained to the toughs. "I have other appointments tonight. Can't you move this thing along?"

"Sack 'em, boss," said the raven.

"You stay out of it, ya ugly crow," the man with the knife warned Jack.

The two toughs advanced slowly, their weapons in their right hands. Equally slowly, their intended victims backed away.

"That's a lovely dance you're all doing," said Toby. "Perhaps you should stop for some punch."

"Like to punch that pig," the tattooed man muttered, and his partner nodded in agreement. They crouched lower and came on.

Barksdale, Tilney, Slatkin, and Chuggers continued to give ground. Soon they were less than ten feet from backing out of the loading doors.

"We can't retreat forever," said Slatkin. "A few more paces and we'll be standing on air."

"We'll have to go for them," Barksdale decided. "Potts, you and the others concentrate on the one with the blackjack. I'll tackle the one with the knife."

"Be careful, sir," said Tilney.

"You be careful where you swings that mallet," Chuggers warned the ferret. "I got enough lumps from this case already."

"Why is nothing happening?" Toby griped to his henchmen. "This isn't the Battle of Waterloo, you know. Stop maneuvering and start murdering them!"

"Murder! Murder!" screamed the raven.

Suddenly, there was a strange sound—a thud, followed by a metallic clinking.

They all turned to look at Toby. To the amazement of everyone—especially Toby—the pig's big head was protruding through the top of his now-battered hat. Perched atop his head was a cloth sack. The seams of the sack had burst, and coins were cascading down both sides of Toby's snout. Sovereigns and shillings pinged and tinkled as they fell to the floor, where a mound of gold and silver was rising around the pig's feet.

"What . . . well . . . hunh," grunted Toby. Then his beady eyes crossed and he toppled over.

"What happened?" asked the man with the knife.

"It's like money from heaven," Chuggers whispered, with awe.

When the two toughs saw Toby unconscious and coins spinning on the floor, they instantly forgot their murderous intentions. Casting aside their weapons, they dove for the money, clawing and punching at each other as they tried to snatch up as many of the coins as possible.

"Stop it!" screeched the raven. "Back to work! Leave the

money!" He hopped onto the shoulders of the wrestling thugs. "Skin the ferret! Skin the ferret!" he croaked, pecking at their ears.

"Shut up, you stinkin' parrot!" yelled the tattooed man. He grabbed the raven by the neck and drove him, beak-first, into a sack of pepper.

"Looks like you been sacked, Jack," said Slatkin, laughing.

The bird wriggled furiously until he was free. Then he turned upon the ferret.

"Skin you myself!" Jack shrieked, flapping madly toward Slatkin. The ferret threw up his arms, backing away.

Suddenly, Jack froze in midair. A queer look came over his feathered face. "Ka-CHOO!" An explosive sneeze spun the bird around. "Ka-CHOO!" Another sneeze blew him by the ferret. The raven sneezed again . . . and again . . . and again—each sneeze like a burst of cannon fire, until a final salvo blew him right through the doorway and out of the wharf.

Before Jack could recover, Slatkin rushed to the doors and slammed them shut. Outside, the vengeful raven battered the planks, alternately scratching, screeching, and sneezing.

"He ought to do something about that condition," Chuggers observed.

"Maybe he should see a taxidermist," the ferret suggested.

Toby's henchmen were so distracted by their greed that it was a simple matter for Chuggers and Barksdale to subdue them. Slatkin tied them both with the doctor's rope. And this time, he made proper knots.

Toby himself was still lying motionless on the floor, a shilling stuck in the end of his snout. The hat brim now encircled the pig's thick neck. "He was right," the hound noted. "My topper does fit him perfectly." Slatkin bound him, too.

"How did it happen, sir?" Tilney wondered. "Where did that money come from?"

"I believe I know the answer," Barksdale replied. He tilted his head back, scanning the rafters. "Fred?" he called. "Fred Hodge, are you there?"

They heard a scuffling noise, then Fred poked his nose over the edge of a beam. "Aye, it's me, sir," he said sheepishly.

"I told you to wait outside, Fred."

"Sorry about that, sir," the rat replied. "I'm afraid I often goes against orders. Just ask my wife."

"This is one instance where I'm very glad you did," Barksdale assured him. "Come down, so we may thank you properly."

Fred slid down a mountain of cinnamon sacks and hopped onto the floor. He bent over Toby. "I never meant to hurt him," he explained. "I was just dragging that sack of coins across the beam, when it slipped off."

"Your aim and timing were perfect," Barksdale declared. "If I were you, I'd say that that was your plan all along and accept the praise for being a hero."

"Hero, sir?" said Fred, with concern. "Oh, no, sir. You mustn't tell people that. If my Nan heard I was acting the hero, well, you know, she'd be proud, at first, but then she'd lecture me something fierce, sir, about risking my neck foolishly and nearly making her a widow with a house full of children. I ain't sure the praise would be worth the penance, sir."

Barksdale chuckled. "Very well, Mr. Hodge. Your courage shall be known only to those of us here, who owe you our lives and are most grateful."

"Which reminds me," Fred continued, looking around the wharf, "where'd that ferret and that bear go to? I wanted to have a few words with them blokes about posing as committee men and playing jokes on honest shopkeepers."

Slatkin and Chuggers were nowhere to be seen.

"They must have slipped away," said Barksdale. "Too bad. I also had a few things to say to them."

"Fred," Tilney asked, "wherever did you get all that money?"

"Sir give it me," Fred answered, pointing toward the hound.

Tilney turned to his master. "Is that true, sir?"

Barksdale looked away. "A very small reward for all that Fred and his family have given me."

Fred picked the coin sack up off the floor. He examined the gaping rents in the fabric. "How shall I ever get all these coins home now? I don't have nothing like enough pockets. 'Course, I never had more money than pockets before."

Taking the tough's knife, the hound slit the top of a sack of cinnamon. He dumped the contents out onto the floor and handed the empty sack to Fred. "There you are. Now you will have the sweetest shillings in all of London."

Barksdale, Tilney, and Fred tossed the coins into the sack, while Toby began to twitch and the two thugs watched in sullen silence.

"I believe our business here is concluded," said Barksdale, when all the coins had been collected.

"What about them?" asked Fred, indicating Toby and his henchmen.

"Leave them to us," said a voice from above.

They raised their heads.

"Nigel!" Tilney exclaimed. "How good of you to come."

Tilney's cousin leaped down from a stack of barrels. He was immediately followed by a dozen other rats, who popped out of crannies in the cargo or dropped silently from the rafters.

"You've had a tough night, cousin," Nigel said to Tilney. "Head on home now and see the family. The boys and I will dump this rubbish on the south side of the river, where it belongs."

"I am indebted to all of you," said Barksdale.

Nigel tipped his cap. "Any friend of Tilney's is a friend of ours. And that means you has lots and lots of friends."

When they were back on the street, Barksdale, who had not slept in thirty-six hours, was suddenly overcome with fatigue. At the first opportunity, he hailed a cab for himself and the two rats.

"Your family will be glad to see you, Potts," said Barksdale, as they squeezed into the seat.

"And to have you back for good and all," added Fred.

There was a moment's uneasy silence in the darkened cab.

"What do you mean, 'for good and all,' Fred?" asked Tilney.

"Uh . . . well . . . I mean . . . it's just . . . your father," stammered Fred.

"Potts," said Barksdale, "I have something to tell you—something as difficult for me to say as it may be for you to hear. And yet, it is something that must be said, for the safety and good of all."

"I can't imagine what that would be, sir," Tilney responded, with obvious concern.

Barksdale took a deep breath. "Potts, I think it would be best if you were to leave my employ."

Again there was a heavy silence in the cab.

"But why, sir?" asked Potts. "Are you displeased with my service?"

"Of course not," Barksdale replied. "Your work is impeccable. You are a servant without equal. In fact, you are indispensable."

"Then why would you dismiss me, sir?"

Barksdale sighed. "I am not dismissing you, Potts. I am protecting you. I fear for your safety. I have placed your life in jeopardy too many times of late. I will not risk it again."

"If there are risks, sir, I incur them willingly."

"It is not for you to decide," was the hound's stern reply. "You are my servant. I may do what I think is best for you."

They rode the rest of the way without speaking. When the hansom reached Fred's address, both rats hopped quickly down from the cab. Barksdale was rising from his seat when Tilney, with a hard edge to his voice, said, "I would like you to wait here, sir."

The hound was surprised and affronted by Tilney's tone, but he sank back onto the cushion without reply.

The two rats moved off into the alley. With his acute night vision, Barksdale was able to follow their actions in the dark. Tilney now engaged in an earnest discussion with Fred. He pulled at his whiskers and gestured angrily as he spoke. Since both rats frequently turned their heads toward the cab, it was obvious to Barksdale that he was the subject of their conversation. And this vexed him.

So we are to part with hard feelings, he fumed, *when there have been no hard feelings between us during all the years we have been together. Well, if that is how it must be. . . .* The hound folded his arms across his chest. *I am sorry to have hurt your feelings, Potts. I am sorry for us both—but it is the correct thing to do. And I gave my word to your father.*

The rats ended their discussion. Fred patted Tilney on the shoulder. They walked down the alley and opened the door to Fred's flat, whereupon they were immediately engulfed by a wave of happy relatives, who hugged them, kissed them, and bore them swiftly inside.

While the rats celebrated Tilney's homecoming, Barksdale brooded in the cab. *I shall have to engage another servant.* The thought made his head ache. *How will I find a servant more suitable than Potts? Who else would do the work of ten servants without complaining? Who else would entertain me with tales of eccentric relatives? Who else would serve a vampire—even a half-vampire—such as I?*

Some time later, Tilney Potts emerged from the flat, accompanied by his sister, Nan, who bore the coin sack over her shoulder.

Barksdale stepped down to greet Mrs. Hodge.

"I wanted to thank you, sir," said Nan. "For the money—which we can't accept—but most of all for bringing Tilney back." She swung the sack off her sturdy shoulder and handed it to the hound.

"But I want you to have it," Barksdale objected.

Nan shook her head. "We have our income, sir. It ain't much, but it keeps us. And we can all work, can't we? There's plenty in this world who ain't able to make a living. You should give this money to them."

"If you and Fred will not accept this for yourselves, then you must take it for your children," the hound protested. "Surely I can do something for them."

Nan pursed her lips, thinking hard. "All right, Mr. Barksdale," she said finally, "you may give them each a coin on their birthdays."

"I shall send a gold sovereign every year," Barksdale promised.

"You shall do nothing of the kind," Nan countered. "You shall bring it yourself, sir—and stay for dinner. For you will always be welcome in our home. Is that agreeable to you?"

Barksdale beamed. "As you wish, Mrs. Hodge."

Nan returned the smile warmly. "We are ever in your debt, sir, for rescuing Tilney."

"I did very little."

"He told us what you were willing to do for him," said Nan. "I would not call that a little thing." Then she raised up on her toes and kissed the hound on the cheek.

Barksdale felt the blood rush to his face.

"I'll come for tea on the usual day," said Tilney to his sister. "And I promise not to speak to strangers on the way." He kissed Nan and hopped into the cab.

"Potts?" Barksdale asked. "I thought you would stay—"

"I have spoken to my father, sir," Tilney replied. "He told me of the promise he extracted from you. I told him that I will always love him, but I must choose my own way in the world."

"But, Potts—your safety . . ."

"How can I ever be in real danger, sir, when I have you to look out for me?"

Barksdale gave his servant a probing glance. "Are you certain about this?" he asked.

"My family will not desert me," the rat replied firmly. "And I will not desert my friends, no matter what you may advise . . . sir."

Barksdale shook his head. "You are a masterful servant, Mr. Potts."

"I am a tired servant, sir. And I should like to go home."

XX

Paid in Full

"And I say Australia," Chuggers declared. He stabbed his forefinger at a gravy stain on the table, as if that amorphous brown spot somehow represented the faraway continent.

Four days had passed since the encounter at Bramstoke Wharf. The ferret and the bear had spent the first two days hiding out in an abandoned building in Clerkenwell, praying that Toby Thigpen and his henchmen would not find them. On the third morning, boredom and hunger had begun to nag at them, so they had decided to risk capture and emerge from their sanctuary. Now they were seated once again in their favorite haunt, the pub called The Jolly Oyster.

"Australia!" cried Slatkin. "Do you know how far away Australia is?"

"'Course I do," Chuggers answered.

"Then how far is it?"

The bear squinted his good eye and screwed up his lips. After a moment, he said, "Very far."

"'Very far?' What kind of answer is that? You don't have no idea where Australia is."

"I know it's very far," said Chuggers. "As for the particulars, I reckon the captain of the ship taking us there will know right enough where to find it, and I'll leave the steering to him."

"Well, it don't matter," Slatkin replied, "'cause I ain't going to Australia."

"Why not?"

"Are you serious? What I want to go live with a bunch of convicts for? You know you can't trust them people. If that's the kind of company I want, I can just march over to Newgate Prison and ask them for a room."

"They'd give you one, too," Chuggers agreed. "But I ain't so sure it wouldn't come with a hangman's noose." They both held that thought for a moment.

"So we ain't going to Australia?" Chuggers asked.

"I ain't going," the ferret confirmed. "If you wants to kiss a kangaroo, that's your business."

"So, what about America?" the bear inquired.

Slatkin shook his head. "My legs is too short for riding a horse. And I ain't going to shoot a buffalo for my dinner."

"Hmm," said Chuggers, sipping his drink. "Is that how it is over there? I thought America were more civilized-like by now."

"Don't you believe it."

"Not even New York City?"

"An oversize trading post on the edge of a wilderness," Slatkin stated emphatically. "Can't hold a candle to London. Probably don't even have a decent pub. And they don't play football in America, neither."

"What do they play?"

"Baseball."

"I heard of it, but I ain't never seen it," said the bear. "What's it like?"

"I ain't sure. Sort of like cricket, I reckon. You bats a ball around. It ain't like football, I can tell you that."

"Still, in America we could make a fresh start," Chuggers suggested. "Lots of people done it already. Think of all them new places to rob. If you works hard, I'll bet you could steal a million dollars."

The ferret shook his head. "*You* can make a fresh start, maybe. I'm too old and tired for fresh starts. All I wants is to avoid a painful finish."

The bear wiped his mouth with the back of his paw. "Well, if you ain't going to America or Australia, where do that leave us, then? Scotland?"

Slatkin shuddered. "Too cold. And them bagpipes sets my teeth on edge."

"Well, we got to go somewhere, don't we?" Chuggers asked. "If we stays here, Toby'll have our hides someday for certain."

"Maybe he will," said Slatkin, plunking his empty glass on the table. "And then again, maybe he won't. This is a big city, ain't it? Didn't we have a devil of a time finding that hound? Maybe Toby's boys will have the same trouble finding us. Maybe, after a while, they'll get tired of looking."

The bear's expression was skeptical. "You don't believe that any more than I do," he argued. "Toby's got the memory of a elephant and more spies than the czar of Russia. He ain't going to let us off the hook, and you knows it."

"All right, then," said Slatkin irritably. "Let the old boar take his revenge. See if I care. I just know this: if I gots to spend the rest of my days looking over my shoulder, I ain't doing it in some foreign country. I'm gonna do it right here in London."

Chuggers picked at his teeth with a claw. "I see what you mean. If we has to take our medicine, might as well take it in our own bed, hey?"

"Exactly," said Slatkin.

There was a lull in the conversation. The bear drummed his paw on the table. The ferret looked at his reflection in the brass lamp hanging above their heads.

"Of course, it wouldn't hurt to lie low for a little while longer," Slatkin suggested. "Give Toby a chance to cool down."

"Exactly," said Chuggers.

"Three or four years in Yorkshire ought to do it."

"Let's go," said Chuggers.

The ferret and the bear were rising from their chairs, when they were both surprised to find the vampire hound standing beside the table.

"What you doing here?" asked Slatkin warily.

"I believe we have some unfinished business, gentlemen," Barksdale said. "Please, sit down."

Slatkin and Chuggers exchanged worried looks, then sagged back into their seats. The hound removed his hat, placing it on the table. Then he, too, sat down.

"How'd you know we was here?" said Slatkin.

"Potts's cousins have been following you since you left Bramstoke Wharf the other night. They told me I would find you here."

"Maybe they ought to be in the detecting business, 'stead of us," Chuggers suggested.

"If you don't mind my asking," the ferret said to Barksdale, "why would you be so interested in finding us? 'Cause I can tell you straight'way—if you is out for revenge, you might have to wait in line."

"This is not about revenge," the hound assured him. "Since you helped to save my life the other night, I thought I should do something for you. Reward you in some way."

"Oh, I couldn't take your money, sir," said Slatkin, raising his paw. "I caused you more grief than a worthy gentleman such as yourself should ever suffer. I don't deserve to be rewarded, just because I discovered a streak of good character in myself there at the end. Of course, I can't speak for Chuggers here. He may take your money. He may not have the same burden of conscience as what I have."

"I got just as much conscience as you," said Chuggers. "Maybe even more. And besides, we is partners, right?"

"Right."

"And friends?"

The ferret nodded.

The bear looked at Barksdale. "Then I can only accept as much as is accepted by my friend and partner, Slatkin, which, in this case, is half of nothing. You is most generous, Mr. Barksdale—but we cannot accept your money."

"I wasn't going to offer you money," said the hound.

Two jaws dropped in disappointment.

"That is too bad." The ferret sighed.

"We was really just being humble-like, Mr. Barksdale," Chuggers explained. "We ain't too honorable to accept money, really, we ain't. Would you like to offer us some?"

"I donate to a great many charitable institutions," the hound replied. "I am not certain that you two belong on that list."

"You is right, of course," said Slatkin. "Forget the reward, sir. We is just thankful you ain't had us thrown in prison, or worse."

"I may not be giving you money," the hound continued, "but I have already done something for you, something you require desperately and cannot refuse."

"How's that?" Slatkin asked.

"Two days ago, through the office of my solicitor, Mr. Church, I sent a sum of money to Mr. Toby Thigpen. My solicitor informed Mr. Thigpen that this money was to be considered payment in full for all debts accrued by Mr. Chuggers and yourself."

"We is paid up?" said Chuggers.

"In full," the hound confirmed.

"Bless you, sir!" said the bear, slapping Barksdale on the back. "You is a good and kind gentleman. Ain't he, Slatkin?"

Slatkin, however, showed no enthusiasm. "Mr. Barksdale, Chuggers and me is extremely grateful for this gesture. Truly we is. But you ought to have saved your money. Just because we don't owe Toby no money, that don't mean he ain't coming after us. Our lives still ain't worth the fleas in Chuggers's trousers."

Reminded by the ferret's remark, the bear began to scratch.

"And besides," Slatkin continued, "you ain't out of danger yourself. Ain't you afraid Toby'll try to get even with you? Ain't you afraid he'll spread your secret all over town?"

"I don't believe Mr. Thigpen knows my secret," said Barksdale, "unless one of you told it to him." He searched the faces of the ferret and the bear.

"He didn't hear it from me," Slatkin asserted. But he stared accusingly at his partner.

"I never said nothing about no vampires to nobody, Toby included," Chuggers declared. "I don't even believe in vampires . . . if you'll pardon my saying it, sir."

"These days, who would believe it?" asked the hound.

"Well, secret or not, Toby'll be after you, Mr. Barksdale," Slatkin stated. "So you might want to make yourself even harder to find than you already is."

"As to that, my communication with Mr. Thigpen also included a warning," the hound explained. "I informed the pig that should he or his associates ever threaten myself, my servant, or anyone connected with me—including the two of you—then he will have to answer, not only to me, but to every rat in this city. As Toby knows, there are thousands and thousands of rats in London. And next time, they may drop the entire Bank of England on him."

"Even half the Bank would do nicely," said Chuggers.

"Yesterday, Mr. Church received a reply from Mr. Thigpen," Barksdale went on. "The pig has accepted both the money and my terms and wishes health and good fortune for all of us."

Slatkin and Chuggers looked at each other, then at the hound.

"You mean . . . we is free and clear?" the ferret asked.

"I believe so," Barksdale replied.

"Then we is most grateful," Slatkin gushed. "Thank you, sir. Thank you very much." He shook Barksdale's paw. Chuggers did the same.

"You are quite welcome, gentlemen. And again, my thanks to you. Now, if you will excuse me . . ." The hound started to rise.

"One second, guv'nuh," Slatkin said. "I know you wasn't planning on giving us money . . . but tell me—if I was to provide you with some information, would that, perhaps, be worth a bob or two?"

"Perhaps. If the information is useful."

"The first bit of news," Slatkin reported, "concerns a certain doctor who has been a certain pain in the neck to certain parties which is present. It seems this doctor did manage to pull himself out of the river the other night, after which he cleared out of London right quick."

"I am aware of that," said the hound. "His house in Chelsea is now empty."

"We know," Chuggers put in. "We tried to burgle it last night."

Slatkin rolled his eyes and groaned. "You big oaf," he muttered. "There weren't no need to tell that."

"Why not?" Chuggers replied. "I thought you was being honest with the gentleman."

"I was, but . . . "

"So I honestly told him we tried to rob the place. Anyways, there weren't nothing to steal, so we ain't guilty of stealing. And I ain't never heard of anyone being charged with not stealing, have you?"

"I was already aware of your attempted burglary," Barksdale revealed. "As for the doctor, he took ship for Sicily two days ago. I trust—I hope—he will not return."

"I'd drink to that . . . if I had another drink," said Chuggers, studying the bottom of his glass.

Barksdale caught the barman's eye and signaled for another round. "Is that all the information you have?"

"There's another bit," Slatkin told him, "which I think you might find of interest, you being so philanthropic and all. To wit—in Kensal Green Cemet'ry, there's a boy and two little ones living in a crypt marked 'Lamie.'"

"They is just orphans," Chuggers assured the hound. "They ain't vampires. They ain't nothin' to be afraid of. Not that vampires is anything to be afraid of," he added.

"If you know the right vampires," Barksdale said.

"Them kids just seem like they could use some help is all," the ferret concluded.

"Have you anything else to tell me?"

Slatkin thought for a minute. "I want to tell you, Mr. Barksdale, that you is the most proper and gentlemanly vampire I ever met. And I hope you is the last vampire I ever meet."

"Thank you, Mr. Slatkin," the hound replied. "I do not pay for compliments, but I will give you something for your tip about the orphans in the cemetery." He removed a five-pound note from his wallet and placed the money on the table. Then he stood up. "It's been a bother doing business with you, gentlemen," he said, with a smile. "I do hope that, in the future, you will find more lawful means of employment. If I can ever be of assistance, feel free to call on me."

"We'll do that, sir," said Slatkin.

"But we still don't know where you lives," Chuggers reminded the hound.

There was a gleam in Barksdale's eye. "I know." With that, he turned and marched out of the pub.

Slatkin and Chuggers watched through the window as the vampire hound disappeared down the street. "Do you think we ought to follow him?" Chuggers asked. "You know . . . sort of wrap up the case?"

Slatkin shook his head. "That detecting work already caused enough trouble for everybody, including us. Besides, he'd only give us the slip."

The barman arrived with two full glasses.

Chuggers raised his drink to Slatkin. The two partners clinked glasses. "I guess we ain't such great detectives," said the bear. "We ain't no Sure Luck Holmes."

"No, friend," the ferret replied, "I guess we ain't."

"But we is certainly a pair," Chuggers added.

Slatkin grinned. "So we is," he said.

Author's Note

Most of the London streets and sites mentioned in this book are still in existence today. To the best of my knowledge, however, there is not now, nor has there ever been, a Harker Lane, Renfield Place, Jolly Oyster pub, or Bramstoke Wharf in London. And all the characters are, of course, fictitious.

J.K.